She love

And it was

Because it _____, ___ canteen gave them a cracker with their Christmas dinner. And Emma somehow managed to find a quiet table near the Christmas tree in the corner—a tree sparkling with tinsel and baubles, with a huge gold star at the top.

Weren't you supposed to make a wish upon a star? And with Christmas being a time of miracles, maybe it would all come true...

Kate Hardy lives in Norwich, in the east of England, with her husband, two young children, one bouncy spaniel, and too many books to count! When she's not busy writing romance or researching local history, she helps out at her children's schools; she's a school governor and chair of the PTA. She also loves cooking—see if you can spot the recipes sneaked into her books! (They're also on her website, along with extracts and stories behind the books.)

Writing for Mills & Boon has been a dream come true for Kate—something she wanted to do ever since she was twelve. She's been writing Medical™ Romances for nearly five years now, and also writes for Modern™ Extra. She says it's the best of both worlds, because she gets to learn lots of new things when she's researching the background to a book: add a touch of passion, drama and danger, a new gorgeous hero every time, and it's the perfect job!

Kate's always delighted to hear from readers, so do drop in to her website at www.katehardy.com

Recent titles by the same author:

In Medical™ Romance—
THE ITALIAN GP'S BRIDE
THE CONSULTANT'S NEW-FOUND FAMILY
THEIR CHRISTMAS DREAM COME TRUE

In Modern™ Extra—
BREAKFAST AT GIOVANNI'S
IN THE GARDENER'S BED
SEEING STARS

Look out for Kate Hardy's sizzling book
ONE NIGHT, ONE BABY
—also out in Modern™ Extra this month!

THE DOCTOR'S VERY SPECIAL CHRISTMAS

BY
KATE HARDY

 **MILLS & BOON**®
Pure reading pleasure

All the characters in this book have no existence outside the imagination of the author, and have no relation whatsoever to anyone bearing the same name or names. They are not even distantly inspired by any individual known or unknown to the author, and all the incidents are pure invention.

First published in Great Britain 2007
Harlequin Mills & Boon Limited,
Eton House, 18-24 Paradise Road, Richmond, Surrey TW9 1SR

© Kate Hardy 2007

ISBN: 978 0 263 85282 0

Set in Times Roman 10¼ on 12¼ pt
03-1207-51726

Printed and bound in Spain
by Litografia Rosés, S.A., Barcelona

For Jo and Sarah, with love

CHAPTER ONE

LIFE didn't get any better than this, Emma thought. A brisk walk in the Peak District on a frosty November morning, when the hills glittered in the winter sunlight and the air was so sharp, so clean, it made your whole body tingle.

Better still, she was on a late shift today so she could do it at sunrise. Watch the deep blue of the sky fade and turn pale pink and yellow at the edges, see the shadows blossom into trees and bushes and rocky folds. Feel the promise of a brand-new day filling her.

A promise she definitely needed today, given that a new registrar was joining the team.

Hopefully he'd fit in to the team as if he'd always been there. Besides, nobody could possibly be worse than Jeremy, his predecessor, who'd come with glowing references and had been the doctor from hell. One who hadn't believed in teamwork, who'd treated the nurses as glorified cleaners and who'd viewed patients as cases rather than people. Jeremy's clinical skills had been good but, without the communication skills to go with them, he'd been a liability to the emergency department. The hospital PR department had probably spent half its time following him around, doing emergency damage limitation.

Robert Howarth had to be better than that.

The department couldn't be that unlucky twice in a row.

Could they?

At the gate, Emma unclipped Byron's lead, and the dog raced to the back door, tail wagging madly. She swallowed the lump in her throat, because she knew exactly what was going to happen next.

And it did. It had been more than a year now, but still Byron looked for Lucy. Ignored his water bowl, went straight into the living room to the sofa and then returned to the kitchen, his plumed tail drooping.

Spaniels always had big sad brown eyes, but right at that moment Byron's looked that little bit sadder. Emma dropped to her knees and ruffled his fur. 'Hey. I miss her, too.' More than missed the big sister who'd always, always been there for her. 'But she'd skin us both for moping. She'd want us to remember her with smiles, not sadness.' All the same, she had to blink away the tears. She rested her cheek against the dog's head. The wide empty space was still there in both their lives. A space that even working a junior doctor's hours and being on the local SARDA team with Byron couldn't fill.

'Motor neurone disease is the pits,' she said fiercely. And she hated the fact it had taken Lucy from her. Lucy, her big sister and best friend. Lucy, who'd practically brought her up, who'd stepped in when their world had fallen apart half a lifetime ago and who'd never complained when her own world had fallen apart for the second time. 'It's so bloody *unfair.* Why did it have to be her?'

The spaniel moved slightly closer, as if agreeing.

Then Emma shook herself. Moping and moaning was completely pointless. It wouldn't bring Lucy back, would it? 'C'mon, gorgeous.' She ruffled his fur again. 'We'll have breakfast. And then I need to hit the shower.'

Lucy's remedy for everything had been a bacon sandwich with tons of tomato ketchup and a mug of tea. Comfort food at its best. And it helped a bit. Emma shared the bacon with Byron, who curled up at her feet, then drained her tea and hit the shower. Three hours until she was due at work, less twenty minutes' travelling. Which gave her enough time to drop in on both sets of elderly neighbours and check they were all right, nip into town to change their library books, call back in at the farm shop in the village for milk and bread, have a cup of tea and a chat with her neighbours, and make her shift on time.

The reception area was already full when Emma walked in. Fine by her: it was just the way she liked it. Though because everyone was busy in cubicles or Resus, it was the middle of the afternoon before she got her first glimpse of Robert Howarth.

And her heart sank.

Because he was the most beautiful man she'd ever seen. Tall, with Celtic colouring—very fair skin, hair so dark it was almost black, and slate-blue eyes.

Stunning good looks in a man went with equally stunning personality defects, in Emma's experience. The sort who bailed out when the going got tough. The sort who'd put himself first, second and third. The sort who bothered about appearances but didn't have the substance to back it up.

The sort she never, ever wanted to get involved with again. Because if she did and her worst fears came true, she knew he wouldn't be there when the sky fell in. He'd walk away, and leave her to deal with it on her own. Just like Damien. Just like Jonathan. And the way he'd already managed to make himself the centre of attention in the staffroom told her that Robert Howarth was definitely a man to keep at a professional distance.

Rob, even though he was chatting to Kirsty and Barbara, two of the emergency department staff nurses, was acutely aware of a woman walking into the staffroom. The feeling of a still, calm space around her. Something that *drew* him.

Weird.

He noticed things, yes, but he never felt drawn to someone like this.

Especially someone who looked quiet and serious.

The best part of six months in plaster had given Rob enough time to learn the lesson and learn it well. Serious was out. Commitment was the quickest way to having your heart stomped on and ground into the dust: he'd been there, done that and didn't want the tour programme, thank you very much. Nowadays, he kept all his relationships light and fun and frothy. And very, very temporary.

This woman—clearly one of the other doctors, judging by the stethoscope around her neck, and who must've been on a late shift because he hadn't been introduced to her on his whistle-stop tour of the department earlier that morning— clearly wasn't the fun and frothy sort. She looked the complete opposite of the frivolous, bubbly women he normally dated. Definitely not his type.

Though she was lovely. Light brown hair caught in a scrun- chie at the nape of her neck, eyes the colour of peridot, and a beautiful mouth that didn't look as if it smiled often enough. A mouth he had the sudden urge to make smile.

But, then, Barbara—whom he'd already pegged as the root of the emergency department grapevine—noticed he was staring and turned round to see what he was looking at.

'Hey, Em! Come over here and meet Rob,' she called.

Em. Was she an Emily, an Emmeline or an Emma? he wondered idly.

He didn't miss the slight disapproval in her expression as she walked over to join them. But why on earth should she disap- prove of him when they'd never met before?

And he was absolutely certain that they hadn't met. He would've remembered.

Barbara introduced them with a beaming smile. 'Rob, this is Emma Russell, our SHO. Em, this is Robert Howarth, our new reg.'

Emma gave him a cool nod. 'Welcome to the department, Dr Howarth.'

He didn't see her frostiness as a challenge, exactly—more that he preferred his working relationships to be easy and friendly. So he simply ignored the chilliness, smiled at Emma and held out his hand. 'Pleased to meet you, Dr Russell. Though I hope you'll call me Rob. I prefer first-name terms: it makes teamwork easier.'

'Rob.' Her smile was a bit on the faint side, but then she took his hand and shook it.

It felt as if an electric shock had jerked through him.

The way her beautiful green eyes widened told him she felt the same—and it was equally unexpected for her.

He had to resist the urge to examine his hand—and hers—for scorch marks.

'I hope you're settling in OK,' she said.

Very polite, no hint of rudeness, but he could tell she'd put up a brick wall between them. Odd. He didn't understand why she would be wary of him.

Then again, everyone in the department had seemed slightly wary of him. They'd been polite rather than welcoming for the entire morning, and he'd had the distinct feeling that Lorraine, the senior sister on the ward, had drawn the short straw for having lunch with him and showing him around. Only now, after the best part of his first shift in the department, had Barbara and Kirsty started to thaw towards him. Rob hadn't quite worked out what was going on, but he'd picked up enough clues to make him suspect something. And he may as well test his theory on Emma Russell. 'If my first day's anything to go by, I'll enjoy working here.' He smiled. 'Though I do hope not all registrars will be tarred with the same brush.'

'I…um…I'm sure they won't.'

The shock in her expression—quickly followed by a flash of guilt—told him that his guess had been spot on. His predecessor had clearly been unpopular. So what had been the problem? Incompetence, blaming his mistakes on his juniors and the nurses? Treating the nurses as his own private little black book?

Whatever, it looked as if he would have to prove himself.

Just as well he liked challenges. Which was why he'd specialised in emergency medicine in the first place.

'I, um…' Emma glanced towards the coffee-machine.

He nodded. 'Breaks are precious. Especially when they involve caffeine. I won't hold you up any longer—and I'm due back in the department anyway. Nice to meet you, Emma. Catch you later, Barbara—Kirsty.' He drained his coffee, rinsed out his mug—and the surprise on everyone's face told him a little more still about their previous registrar—and headed back to the ward.

His next case took his mind off Emma: a white-faced boy with his arm in a home-made sling constructed by someone who'd clearly done this before. A woman was talking to a little girl at the same time as reassuring the boy.

A quick glance at the triage nurse's assessment—and the attached set of notes—made him wince. Poor kid. It looked as if he was the accident-prone type: one of those who ended up in Casualty frequently enough to be flagged as a potential abuse case. Though Rob could already see by the way the mother was interacting with the kids that this definitely wasn't abuse.

'Hi, I'm Dr Robert Howarth.' He smiled at them. 'Tom, can I have a look at your arm?'

The boy nodded.

'I'm going to touch your arm as gently as I can. Tell me when I touch somewhere that hurts.' He gently removed the sling, then checked the pulse points from the elbow downwards.

As soon as he got to the boy's wrist, Tom flinched. 'Ow. It stings there.'

'Can you bend your fingers for me?'

Just, but the flicker of pain on Tom's face made Rob suspect a fracture.

'And can you move your wrist like this?' Rob demonstrated, flexing his own wrist so his flat palm was at ninety degrees to his arm, then pushing it down again as far as he could.

Tom tried, but his sharp intake of breath made Rob stop him. 'OK, Tom. You don't have to do that any more, because it obviously hurts. Want to tell me what happened?'

The boy's lower lip wobbled. 'I was roller-skating.'

'I said he had to wait until it had thawed out a bit.' Tom's mother sighed. 'Except Tom's not very good at waiting. I thought he was messing about with the dog in the garden.'

'I only skated a *little* bit,' Tom protested. 'I fell.'

'Flat on his face. On the patio,' his mother confirmed.

Rob could guess what had happened next. 'And you put out a hand to save yourself?' he asked Tom.

The boy nodded.

'It's really common. Adults do it a lot, too, especially when it's icy outside,' he reassured Tom. 'I think what you've done is what's called a Colles' fracture. We've had six people in with one of those today already.'

'Six?'

'Uh-huh. So you're probably going to be lucky number seven.'

'I don't feel very lucky,' Tom muttered.

No, poor little mite. Rob knew just what bone pain was like.

'I'm going to give you something to take the pain away,' Rob said, 'and then I'll send you for an X-ray. If I'm right, I'm afraid you'll be in plaster for a month.'

Tom's mother sighed. 'He's only been out of plaster for a few weeks! Still, at least it's not his writing arm this time.' She ruffled the boy's hair. 'So that's no football and no swimming for *another* six weeks. Sorry, honey.'

'Sounds as if you know the drill,' Rob said with a smile as he gave Tom pain relief.

'Yup. This is the third time he's broken his arm this year,' she said, looking rueful. 'The first two times were at school— once in the playground and once at football. And I think those roller-boots are going away until the spring.'

'Oh, *Mum*!' Tom looked horrified. 'But Dad—'

'No buts,' she said firmly. 'It's winter, it's icy, and we'll wait until the ground's a bit softer. And you'll put knee and elbow pads on next time before you use them.'

'I take it you know where X-Ray is, then?' Rob asked.

She nodded. 'We go to Reception and tell them we're here, wait until he's called, then come back here for the results?'

'Yes. And then, once I've reviewed the X-rays, if I'm right about the fracture, he'll be off to the plaster room. A fibre-glass cast for a month, and a couple of weeks taking things very easy.'

Tom looked utterly downcast, and his mother gave him a hug. 'Hey, Tom, it's not so bad. In my day, they used to be really heavy casts. Like that backslab you had to wear overnight last time. And it used to be kept on for at *least* six weeks. And you'll still be able to use your games console. Come on, sweetheart.' She shepherded the children out of the cubicle. 'I think we're going to be playing I Spy for just a bit longer…'

Rob saw another two patients before Tom's X-rays arrived. The moment he put it on the lightbox, he could see it was a classic Colles' greenstick fracture. He called Tom's mother back in. 'Can you spot it here?' he said to Tom, pointing out the fracture on the X-ray.

'It's so little,' Tom said in amazement. 'You can hardly even see it!'

'Still hurts, though,' Rob said.

'Supposing it'd been a *big* crack?'

'Ah, now, they hurt even more,' Rob said with a grimace. 'Especially if it's both legs and both arms.'

Tom's eyes were round as he looked at Rob. 'Is that what *you* did?'

He nodded. 'About five years ago, when I was climbing.' Though it hadn't been his bones that had taken longest to heal. He pushed the thought away and gave Tom's mother a quick smile. 'Which I would guess your mum wouldn't want you to try.'

Tom's mum groaned. '*Definitely* not! Come on, Tom. Back to the plaster room—and we can see what colours they have today.'

'I want a blue one. Like my favourite football club,' Tom said immediately.

'Just like the last two, hmm? And everyone can sign it at school when term starts again next week.' She smiled at Rob. 'Thanks for sorting him out.'

'No worries. That's what I'm here for.'

It wasn't that often you got thanks—sometimes patients were in too much pain or too upset for it to cross their minds—and Rob was still smiling when he walked through the cubicles area, ready to see the next patient on the list.

And then he heard a voice he recognised.

A voice that was soft and sweet, with none of the coolness or wariness he'd heard in the rest room.

Just then the curtains twitched open and he caught a glimpse of an elderly lady with the most horrendous black eye. And Emma's face was filled with worry.

'Anything I can do?' he asked as she stepped away from the cubicle.

She shook her head. 'Probably not.'

He lowered his voice. 'Want me to call the police?'

She frowned. 'Why?'

Did she really need to ask? 'Because your patient looks as if she's just been mugged,' he pointed out.

She shook her head. 'Mrs Johnson comes from a village in the Peak District, not an inner city.'

He frowned. 'Are you trying to tell me you have a zero crime rate in the Peak District?' Ridiculous. He didn't believe that for a second.

'No, but people tend to look out for each other in the villages.' There was a definite warning note in her tone, then her face softened slightly. 'You're more used to inner-city medicine?'

He nodded. 'I worked at London City General for the last four years.'

'At Fellside General, as well as covering part of the Sheffield area, we cover a few villages in the Peak District—like the one where Mrs Johnson lives,' Emma explained.

'So what happened?'

'She fell and caught her head on the side of the table. Luckily the window-cleaner was there that afternoon. When he was cleaning the kitchen windows he saw her lying on the floor, so he went in to her and called the ambulance.' She sighed. 'Even though her sight's fine and that shiner's going to fade, my guess is that she's not able to manage on her own any more. She's eighty-five.'

'So what are you going to do?' Rob asked.

'Get her an OT and physio assessment. I need to know why she fell—if it was something she needs medication for or whether she just tripped and needs a proper risk assessment on her home to sort out potential problems before she gets hurt again.' She bit her lip. 'I hate cases like this, where someone's got sixty years of memories in a house and we threaten to take it all away because of one little fall. She's clearly scared that's what's going to happen because she doesn't want us to call her daughter.'

'She doesn't necessarily have to move,' Rob said.

Emma blinked in surprise. 'How do you mean?'

'We get independent people in London, too. People who're still living in the house they were born in—maybe they survived the war there too, so they're not going to give up. The occupational therapists can help a lot—as you say, do an assessment of the house and find out what she needs. The first thing is to make sure she has an alarm—the sort you wear around your neck.'

'Got one. Doesn't wear it.' Emma sighed. 'She doesn't think she needs it.'

'Want me to try talking to her?' Rob asked.

She looked at him. 'You?'

He raised an eyebrow. 'Why do you sound so surprised?'

She shrugged. 'I didn't think you'd be interested.'

That cool disdain stung. Badly. And the fact that it rattled him annoyed him even more. Working together didn't mean they had to like each other. He shouldn't care what Emma Russell thought. All the same, he couldn't help asking, 'You don't like me, do you?'

She spread her hands. 'It's not my job to like you—just to work with you.'

Exactly what he'd just told himself. He knew he should leave it there, not try and push things—for goodness' sake, this was his first day in the department and it'd be stupid to start making waves this soon—but he wanted this sorted. Right here, right now. 'I've got news for you, Smiler,' he said, his voice very soft. 'I'm a registrar, yes, but we're not all the same kind of person.'

'I don't know what you mean.'

Oh, yes, she did. He resisted the urge to grit his teeth.

'Clare in Reception filled me in about my predecessor about fifteen minutes ago—after I asked her a direct question. And it would save a lot of time if I didn't have to prove to you—and the rest of the department, for that matter—that although I'm doing Jeremy's job now, I'm not Jeremy.' He left a deliberate pause between each of the last three words. Maybe that would help the message sink in. And, just in case it didn't, he added, 'I'd appreciate it if you could get that into your head.'

Colour rose in her cheeks. Good. He'd made his point. Hopefully she'd remember it and things would be smoother in from now on. Working in a busy emergency department, he had quite enough to deal with—he didn't need to cope with other people's prejudices as well.

'Now. Your patient's name?' he asked.

'Mrs Johnson.'

'OK.' He walked back into the cubicle. 'Hello, Mrs Johnson. My name's Rob. I work with Emma.'

'Oh, aye.'

'That eye looks painful.'

'Just a bruise,' the old lady said. 'Dr Russell here checked and there's nothing wrong with my eyes. I can see perfectly all right.'

'That's good.' He smiled at her.

'I'm all right now, and you've got people waiting to see you. Can I go home?'

He shook his head. 'Not until we've done some assessments.'

Mrs Johnson's mouth pursed. 'If you're on my daughter's side and trying to stick me in a home, I'm not going. I've lived in that cottage all my married life and I'm not going to leave it now.'

'Of course you're not,' Rob said. 'That's why we want to do the assessments.'

'If it's a medical condition that made you fall, we can treat it. And as well as that the occupational therapist can take a look at your home and see what can be done to make your life easier,' Emma chipped in.

Mrs Johnson didn't look at all convinced. 'I'm perfectly all right. I can manage.'

'That's what my gran said,' Rob said with a smile. 'But I bullied her into having an assessment done. And afterwards she had to admit that just having her chair raised about four inches made it a lot easier for her to get out of it. Just little changes like that can do so much to make your life easier—why struggle and make it hard for yourself when you don't have to?'

'Your gran?' Mrs Johnson queried.

'Yes. She's eighty-seven and still going strong in the same house she's lived in as far back as I can remember. Seeing the OT meant she could keep her independence. Yes, there were little changes around the house—nothing too obvious, but they made her life easier and meant she didn't have to move. Though she did have to compromise on one thing,' he added.

'What's that?' Mrs Johnson asked suspiciously.

'Wearing one of those alarms around her neck. She said she didn't need one because she was always near a phone and she carried a cordless one around with her. But as I said to her, if she tripped and fell and hurt herself or knocked herself out, and the phone happened to land out of her reach, she probably wouldn't be able to drag herself to the phone—and these alarms are brilliant. If you fall, you don't even have to press a button because there's a little sensor that can tell what happened and sends the alarm signal for you.' Rob spread his hands. 'So Gran promised to wear it. She's never actually had to use it, but it's given the family peace of mind. We don't have to worry about her the way we did before she had the alarm. So that means we've all stopped nagging her and driving her bananas—and when we see her we can all enjoy the time together instead of grilling her about how she's managing and making a fuss.'

Mrs Johnson looked thoughtful. 'So if I wear one of those alarm things, I can stay in my home and people aren't going to try and make me move?'

'That, and any little changes the occupational therapist thinks would help you,' Emma said softly.

'Hmm. Well, I'll think about it.'

'You do that,' Rob said with a smile. 'Emma's going to arrange the assessment for later this afternoon. Can I get you a cup of tea?'

'Thanks, that'd be nice.' The old lady nodded. 'Strong, one sugar, only a tiny bit of milk.'

'Coming right up, Mrs Johnson.'

Emma followed him out of the cubicle. 'You're going to make a patient a cup of tea?'

'Yes. Got a problem with that?'

'No. It's just…' Her voice faded.

He could guess exactly what she hadn't said—and said it for her. 'Jeremy never did it.' Oh, for goodness' sake. He'd already told her he wasn't like their previous registrar. Did she expect him to go through hoops to prove it? He felt his face tighten. 'Don't tell me—he clicked his fingers and told the nearest nurse to do it, and look sharp about it?'

'Something like that,' she said dryly.

Rob rolled his eyes. 'Don't tar us all with the same brush. If I bring Mrs Johnson that cup of tea the way she likes it, she's going to know I listened to her. Which means she's going to trust me. And if she trusts me, that means she's going to let me help her. So making that cup of tea for her myself is just as important as sending blood samples for the usual tests. As is giving children bravery stickers and learning terrible jokes to distract them when you want to give them an injection.'

'I'm sorry,' Emma said.

He tried to damp down just how gratified he felt by that quiet apology. As if he'd won a major, major victory. He knew he still had a long way to go before he was accepted here. But maybe it was his turn to compromise. 'We got off on the wrong foot. It happens. Let's start again.' He held out his hand. 'Robert Howarth—known to most people as Rob, and to kids as Dr Rob. Pleased to meet you.'

She took his hand and shook it. Again, there was that fizz of energy between them, the unexpected flutter in his stomach. She was the one to break the contact: just as well, because otherwise he might have been too tempted to yank her into his arms and kiss her.

Sexual attraction. That was all it was. Pheromones. Something that would pass.

And it had better pass quickly, before he did something stupid. No way did he want to get involved.

'Emma Russell. Known to most people as Emma, and to kids as Dr Em.' She gave him a level stare. 'Not "Smiler".'

Ah. So she *had* heard him. And it had clearly rankled. 'If I apologise for being sarcastic, will you smile for me?' he asked.

Her eyes widened. 'Smile?'

He knew it was crazy, but he really wanted to see her smile. 'Just a little one?'

She coughed. 'You haven't apologised yet.'

'OK. I'm sorry for being sarcastic to you,' he said softly. 'It was sheer bad manners—and bad temper, because I don't like people judging me before they know me, and the fact you did it rubbed me up the wrong way. But I realise that two wrongs don't make a right, and I shouldn't have reacted the way I did. Now do I get a smile? Please?'

'OK.' A small one. One that actually reached her eyes this

time. And Rob wished he hadn't teased her into it when his whole body started to tingle.

If he wasn't careful, he could find himself falling for Emma Russell.

Which went against everything in his personal rulebook.

CHAPTER TWO

EMMA couldn't get Rob Howarth out of her head.

Even a seriously busy afternoon in cubicles didn't distract her. She still kept seeing those slate-blue eyes, that beautiful mouth.

Worse still, she actually found herself speculating what it would feel like to have that mouth brushing against her skin, exploring, discovering the places she liked to be—

No.

OK, so Rob wasn't like Jeremy. The way he'd dealt with Mrs Johnson had proved that. The cup of tea hadn't been for show either, because he'd used it as an excuse to chat to Mrs Johnson and get her to admit to some of the things she found difficult. She'd seen his handwriting on the notes for the OT—things Mrs Johnson definitely hadn't spoken about in front of Emma.

But that was work.

Outside work was a completely different matter.

And Emma wasn't planning to get involved with anyone. Been there, done that, crashed spectacularly, and didn't repeat her mistakes. Damien had cured her of any romantic notion she'd ever held. He'd left her to deal with things on her own, just when she'd needed his support most. And she wasn't ever going to let herself get in that position again.

Even if Robert was the most gorgeous man she'd ever met.

The first man in years she'd actually noticed as a man, not just as a colleague.

Stop it, she told herself. You should know better than that.

If only Lucy were here. Calm, sensible Lucy who'd smile, sit her down with a mug of coffee and a huge bar of chocolate, and talk some sense into her, the way she had during Emma's teens.

But she was on her own now. So she'd just have to deal with it.

She grabbed five minutes for a coffee-break and had just drained her mug when Rob walked into the rest room.

And her whole body tingled with the memory of how it had felt when he'd taken her hand.

A simple handshake really shouldn't be that memorable. She needed to get a grip. Preferably right now. Before she said something unutterably stupid.

'Hi.' He smiled at her. 'I'm really glad I caught you, Emma.'

Was he? 'Why?'

'I'm having a drink in town with some of the team tonight. We're probably going to a club afterwards. I know you're on a late, but why don't you come along when you've finished your shift?' He took a pad from the pocket of his white coat, scribbled a number on it, ripped off the top sheet and handed it to her. 'My mobile phone number. Call me when you're ready to join us and I'll tell you where we are.'

Emma couldn't exactly refuse the piece of paper or crumple it into a ball and throw it in the bin. She wasn't *that* rude. And although she was very, very tempted to say yes, no way was she going to make the mistake of letting him close. 'Thanks for the invite, but I'm afraid I can't.'

'Your boyfriend doesn't like you going on team nights out?' he guessed.

Did he think she was some kind of doormat? Even when she'd been engaged to Damien, she hadn't asked 'how high' whenever he'd told her to jump. She lifted her chin. 'It isn't that.'

'What, then?'

She could hardly tell him it was because he was the most amazing-looking man she'd ever seen and she didn't trust herself not to do something stupid. Like allowing him into her life. Like risking him letting her down, the way Damien had let her down and Jonathan had let Lucy down. 'I'm just not into pubs and clubs,' she hedged.

He shrugged. 'Suit yourself. If you change your mind, you're welcome to come along. Catch you later.'

And then he was gone.

Emma added cold water to her coffee so she could drink it straight down for a caffeine hit.

Robert Howarth had asked her out.

But it had been a general invite along with the team, not a proper date. She had to keep that in mind. And now the grapevine had finally come up with the gossip on Robert Howarth, she knew he was a dedicated party-lover who never dated anyone more than twice. Completely unreliable—even more so than Damien. So she'd keep it cool. Colleagues. And no hint of anything more.

Maybe she should tell him the rest of it. About Lucy. About the genes that might spell disaster. She was pretty sure that'd send him running even faster than Damien had.

But then again, Robert Howarth had a kind side. He'd proved that by the way he'd helped Mrs Johnson. So maybe he wouldn't run if she told him. Maybe, she thought, her stomach sinking, it'd be worse than that.

Because she really didn't want to see pity in Rob's eyes when he looked at her.

The next morning, Emma was in Resus on an early shift. And so was Rob.

To her relief, he didn't make any comment about the fact she hadn't turned up last night. And it wasn't as if she'd stood him up—she'd told him right from the start she wasn't going. And it hadn't been a date anyway.

But that tingling feeling at the base of her spine was still there every time she looked at him. And when he handed her a cup of coffee in the rest room and her fingers touched his, she nearly dropped the mug.

What on earth was wrong with her? She was known for being level-headed and sensible. She was on her way to becoming a registrar herself, for goodness' sake—she wasn't some giddy teenager who blushed and giggled whenever a handsome boy smiled at her.

Though there wasn't anything boyish about Rob Howarth.

He was all man.

Oh, dear. She had to stop thinking like this or she was going to go crazy.

Luckily her next patient was enough to get her mind firmly back on the subject of work. Even though she was seeing him with Rob.

'This is Jason,' Keith, the paramedic, told them. 'Aged eighteen. Diabetic.'

The boy's pallor really wasn't a good sign.

'His mum says he's been burning the candle at both ends. His pulse is a hundred and twenty.'

Way higher than it should be: clearly he was dehydrated and because that meant his blood was thicker than usual, his heart had to pump faster to push the blood through his veins.

'His tongue's really dry and his blood pressure's not good,' Keith continued. 'We've started him on saline.'

'Good,' Emma said. It would help get his blood pressure and

pulse back to normal—though at the same time there was a fine balance. If they replaced the fluid too fast, there was a risk that Jason would go into cardiac failure or suffer cerebral oedema—complications they could really do without.

The moment Keith finished the handover, Rob glanced at Emma. 'OK. You lead, I'll back you up.'

He was letting her lead? Now, there was a surprise. Jeremy had never, ever let anyone else lead.

Rob clearly guessed that, because he gave her an extremely cheeky wink. 'Tut—tut, Smiler. Tempted to tar me with the same brush again?'

The nickname hit a raw nerve. 'Careful. I might be tempted to add feathers.' And she wasn't entirely joking.

He laughed. 'Is that an offer?'

But before she could come back with an equally smart retort, Rob put a gentle hand on Jason's shoulder. 'How are you feeling, mate?'

'Terrible,' the boy slurred. 'Tired. Shouldn't've been out s'late last night, that's all. Didn't need ambulance.' Then Jason took a sharp intake of breath.

'Where does it hurt?' Rob asked.

Jason's face was white. 'All over.'

'I'm not going to lecture you about taking your insulin properly—women are much better at nagging, so Dr Russell here will do that,' he added with a smile, 'but we're going to check you over now, do some tests and get you some pain relief, OK?'

Jason swallowed hard and nodded.

'Right, Em. Talk me through this,' Rob said, turning to Emma.

'We need to get Jason's blood pressure and pulse back to normal quickly, but without replacing the fluid too fast because I don't want to risk complications. Jason, can I ask you, have you been weeing a lot lately?'

Jason nodded. 'Last couple of days.'

'Anything else that's made you feel a bit off colour the last few days?'

He shook his head. 'Been out late with my mates a couple of times—and I have to be up early for work.'

'OK. I'm going to check your glucose levels, and I'm going to take a blood sample so we can check the level of various chemicals that might need sorting out. You've already got a drip in your hand so we can get some fluids into you and make you feel a bit better—I'll give you some insulin the same way,' she said. 'Now, you'll feel a sharp scratch—hardly anything—OK?'

'Yeah,' he whispered.

'Well done.' She smiled at him, then turned to Rob. 'He's breathing deeply and rapidly, and his breath smells of pear drops. I think we're looking at diabetic ketoacidosis.'

'I agree,' Rob said. 'Which tests are you going to do?'

'Us and Es, full blood count, electrolyte balance and glucose on the bloods—and I'd like a chest X-ray and an ECG as well. I'd also like cultures on the blood as well as urine to check there isn't an infection. I think it's probably due to insufficient insulin, but I want to check out the rest of the four Is as well.' Infection, infarction—even though Jason was young—and intercurrent illness. The body reacted to illness and infection by releasing more glucose into the bloodstream, stopping insulin from working properly: and consistently high blood glucose levels meant that DKA—diabetic ketoacidosis—could develop.

Rob smiled at her. 'Spot on. I'll write up the labels for you, then.'

She squeezed Jason's hand. 'You're going to feel a lot better soon. I know you're feeling rough right now, but could you do me a urine sample?'

Jason's face turned bright red. 'What, *here*?'

She smiled. 'I won't look. But I need to do a quick test of

your glucose levels so I know how much insulin to give you. So I need you to wee into this for me.' She handed him a bottle.

A couple of minutes later she tested the sample with a dipstick and nodded. 'Yup, your sugar's way out of whack. It's over fifteen millimol per litre.' She sorted out the insulin drip. 'Now, I know you think I'm going to nag you...'

Jason groaned. 'Yeah.'

'Well, you're wrong. I don't think I need to nag you—because my guess is you really won't want to feel this terrible in future.'

He pulled a face. 'No.'

'So you don't need me to tell you that if you don't sort out your insulin properly, this'll happen again and again. Right now you have something called diabetic ketoacidosis. What it means is your blood glucose levels are high, so your body can't use the glucose for energy and has to use fat stores instead. The byproduct is called ketones—that's why your breath smells of pear drops—and your body's trying to get rid of the ketones by making you wee them out, so you're getting dehydrated. Because you're dehydrated, your body's finding it much harder to get rid of the ketones and the levels keep rising faster than your body can get them out. It's a vicious circle. That's why you're feeling so rough right now,' she explained. 'And long term you could be putting yourself at risk of a heart attack, as well as problems with your kidneys and your eyes.'

'Yeah.'

She smiled at him. 'How long have you been diabetic?'

'Since I was seven,' he told her, pulling a face.

'Are any of your mates diabetic?'

He shook his head.

'It's hard,' she said softly, 'when you want to live your life just like everyone else and you feel you're different. But if you keep on top of the insulin, you can live a really normal life. If you can accept it, your mates will too because it's part of you.'

Jason grimaced. 'I'm always going to be stuck with the kit. Having to stick a needle in me all the time.'

'True. But knowledge is power,' she said. 'You can let this beat you. Or you can find out as much as you can about diabetes and how your body works—so *you're* in charge, not the diabetes.'

'I never thought of it that way,' Jason said.

'It's up to you,' she said with a smile. 'I'm not going to nag you. But I can definitely get someone to come and have a chat with you, if you want.'

He nodded. 'Please.'

'No worries.'

Rob definitely liked the way Emma worked. She looked at the big picture and she saw the person, not a case. She'd been good with Mrs Johnson yesterday, reassuring her that nobody was going to stick her into a home. And today she'd been great with the teenager, who could've been stroppy and uncooperative— she'd got him to look at his condition a different way, accept it more, so in the future he was less likely to have the same problem. In time, she'd make a superb registrar—and an extremely capable consultant.

The more Rob saw of her, the more he liked.

And the more he wanted to break his personal rule and get to know her better.

'Have lunch with me?' he asked when they left Resus to go to the staffroom.

She shook her head. 'Thanks for the offer, but I can't—I need to run a few errands.'

Her expression gave her away: she didn't have to run errands at all. Or, if she did, they weren't that urgent. It was an excuse.

And not a particularly convincing one. 'If I were a paranoid man, Emma Russell, I'd say you were avoiding me,' he said, deliberately keeping his voice light. He knew that if he was too confrontational, it would make things even worse between them.

She flushed. 'Of course I'm not. We work together.'

'Last night you wouldn't come out for a team drink.'

'I was on a late. I was tired.'

He could just about buy that one. But not the excuse she'd just given him. 'And today you're too busy to have lunch with me.' He paused. 'Is there a problem I need to know about?'

She lifted a careless shoulder. 'I don't have a problem with you.'

He knew she wasn't telling the truth. If she was, she wouldn't be avoiding him, would she? 'Then have lunch with me—and I'll help you run your errands afterwards,' he suggested.

She shook her head. 'Sorry. I really am busy.'

'Then have dinner with me tonight, instead.' He knew she was going to say no and hoping to forestall it he added, 'I'm new to the area and you know it well. I could do with someone to give me the heads up.'

'Sorry. Prior commitments.'

Another non-specific excuse. She hadn't suggested an alternative. And he'd noticed that she tensed up whenever he was near: what exactly was the problem here? 'Are you scared of me?' he asked softly as they walked into the staffroom.

She frowned. 'Don't be ridiculous.'

Guessing wasn't working. He may as well ask her straight. Get it out into the open—so they could deal with it, put it behind them and move forward. 'Then what's the problem, Emma?'

She spread her hands. 'You're the partying type, I'm not.'

She was taking the holier-than-thou stance now? Oh, for pity's sake. It wasn't as if he'd ever been hungover on a shift, or turned up late and let the team down because he couldn't be bothered to get out of bed with his current lover.

And what was wrong with having fun, anyway? He forgot about being gentle. Emma Russell was way too serious. She needed to lighten up. 'Ever thought about letting your hair down?'

'You know that's against the hygiene regulations at work. Long hair's meant to be tied back.'

He felt his eyes narrow. 'And you know I was speaking metaphorically.'

She shrugged. 'I'm fine as I am.'

No, she damn well wasn't. Whatever the problem between them, they needed to get it sorted. Sooner rather than later. 'OK. It's no to a drink, no to lunch and no to dinner.' He paused. 'We're on the same team so I know your shifts are the same as mine—which means you're off on Sunday morning.' Maybe, just maybe, a different tack would work here. Maybe Emma was an outdoor girl. 'How about coming climbing with me?'

She stared at him, her eyes wide. Shock? Fear? He couldn't tell.

'You climb for *fun*?' she asked.

'Doesn't everyone around here? We're on the edge of the Peak District—it's gorgeous.' And a fantastic area for climbing. Rob planned to explore every single bit of it while he was off duty.

Emma's face had gone slightly white. 'I don't climb for fun.'

Definitely the wrong tack, then. Climbing wasn't everyone's cup of tea. It certainly hadn't been Natasha's. She'd had exactly the same expression on her face as Emma had now, when he'd suggested she joined him on a climb. Right at that moment Natasha and Emma could've been twins.

He pushed the thought aside. He was *not* going to think about his ex-fiancée. Not after all this time. He was over her. He'd moved on. He knew he was much better off on his own—

or with female company who didn't expect their relationship to turn permanent.

Not that he had a relationship with Emma.

And he didn't have a clue what she wanted from him. Only that he was sure she felt that same strange pull and was fighting it just as hard.

He knew he should just leave it, but he couldn't. His mouth ran away with him before he could stop the words coming out. 'So what do you do for fun, then?'

She folded her arms, clearly taking it that he was suggesting she didn't know how to have fun. 'I don't have to prove myself to you.'

But she'd expected him to prove to her that he wasn't like Jeremy, the previous registrar. He kept his gaze locked on hers. No way was he letting her off the hook that easily.

And he refused to ask himself why it mattered so much. Refused even to consider the idea that he'd just let it go if she were anyone else.

'I'm not asking you to prove yourself—just wondering what you do for fun.'

She sighed. 'Look, Rob, we're very different. The sort of things I do for fun, you'd find boring.'

All sorts of ideas spilled into his head—ideas that made his heart miss a beat. Ideas that no way could he act on right now. But she'd given him an opening, an opportunity he wasn't going to let slip by. 'Try me,' he said quietly.

She shook her head. 'We work together. And that's it.'

Why was she so insistent on keeping this professional distance between them? She barely knew him, so she couldn't be wary of him personally. Maybe she'd been hurt before. As badly as he had. 'You're scared of men?' he guessed.

She gave him a scathing look. 'Don't be ridiculous.'

'You've got a possessive boyfriend who doesn't like you talking to anyone of the opposite sex?'

She rolled her eyes. 'No.'

'Have you got a boyfriend at all?'

She looked away. 'That's a personal question.'

No,' he corrected, 'it's a colleague being friendly and trying to get to know you a bit better.' Not strictly true, but he didn't dwell on that. 'If a female doctor had asked you that question, you would've answered it, yes?'

She shrugged. 'I suppose.'

'So what's the difference between me asking and a woman asking?'

She coughed. 'Tut-tut, Dr Howarth. Don't tell me you've forgotten your basic anatomy.'

Emma wished she hadn't teased him when his gaze grew hot.

It was her own fault. She'd just reminded him that she was a woman and he was a man. And she knew from the expression on his face at that precise moment that he was thinking about kissing her.

Just as she was thinking about what it would be like if he kissed her.

This shouldn't be happening.

But she couldn't stop the idea running through her head.

It would be, oh, so easy to slide her arms around his neck and draw his head down to hers. Brush her lips against that beautiful mouth. Nibble at his lower lip until he let her deepen the kiss. Press her body against his, her soft warmth against his hard muscles. And—

Oh, for goodness' sake, she needed to get a grip. This was the staffroom. Not the place for indulging in fantasies she had no intention of acting on.

'I need to run those errands,' she muttered. 'I'll see you later.' She grabbed her bag from her locker and left the room virtually at a run, not giving him the chance to suggest coming with her.

Rob stared after her. Oh, lord. He was in trouble now. *Basic anatomy.* The thoughts in his head right now were very, very basic indeed. And they were probably written all over his face. No wonder she'd left the room so fast.

This wasn't a personality clash. There was definitely something between them. Something she was resisting even more than he was.

And right at that moment he didn't have the faintest idea how to sort it out.

CHAPTER THREE

'THIS is stupid,' Emma told Byron as she took him for a walk before her early shift on Thursday morning. 'I should know better, especially after Damien.'

The advantage of talking to her dog was that he couldn't answer back—or tell her just how ridiculous she was being.

'Robert Howarth is *so* not my type.'

And it drove her crazy that she couldn't stop thinking about him. They'd been working together for three days now. And even though she'd been trying to see him as just another doctor, her body refused to listen to her head. Her awareness of Rob had grown and grown and grown—to the point that every time she accidentally brushed against him or caught his eye her temperature seemed to go up about ten degrees.

Her dreams left her even more hot and bothered. She needed a cold shower before she could even set foot in the hospital.

'This sort of thing shouldn't happen to me. I'm sensible. I'm a doctor.'

Byron nudged her knee, as if to remind her that she was only human.

Ha. Although the dog was too sweet-natured to growl or show his teeth, he'd taken an instant dislike to Damien and had refused to go anywhere near the man. 'I bet you'd avoid Robert Howarth, too,' she said.

Though she couldn't avoid him. Not only were she and Rob working the same shifts, they were working on the same team. They were rostered in cubicles that morning and despite the fact that there was a curtain between them she was all too aware of his presence. All her senses seemed attuned to him. And although she managed to do her job competently, she knew her mind wasn't completely on what she was doing—because she was thinking about Rob.

Her fourth case that morning was a postman who'd been bitten by a dog.

'Hazard of the job?' she asked.

He looked rueful. 'Yes, but I wasn't even at work! It's my neighbour's. It's a vicious little thing—and it hates me. I'd gone out to put some rubbish in the bin, and it took exception to that.'

'In your garden?'

'There's a hole in the fence between me and next door— which I'll be blocking up as soon as I get home again, believe you me.' He rolled his eyes. 'That'll teach me to go out in a T-shirt instead of full body armour.'

'It's pretty deep,' Emma said. 'I'll give you a local anaesthetic first, and then I'll take a proper look.' When the anaesthetic had taken effect, she explored the bite. 'I can't see any foreign body in there, so your neighbour's dog is still armed with a full set of teeth.'

He grimaced. 'Oh, wonderful.'

'Better than having one in your arm that I have to get out. The bite's in the middle of your arm so there isn't any joint involvement, and I don't think there's a fracture so I'm not going to send you for an X-ray. What I'll do is clean the area thoroughly.'

'Stitches?' he asked.

She shook her head. 'It's a deep puncture wound and I don't want it to get infected. I'm going to give you some antibiotics so hopefully it'll stop your arm getting inflamed. Are you allergic to penicillin?'

'No.'

'Good.' She smiled. Co-amoxiclav was a broad-spectrum antibiotic that worked well in this sort of case, unless the patient was allergic to penicillin. 'When was your last tetanus injection?'

He frowned, then shook his head. 'Can't remember.'

'To be on the safe side, I'm going to start you on a tetanus course. You'll need to see your GP for a booster and I'd like you to make a follow-up appointment with your GP for tomorrow afternoon—if you're going to have any problems with your arm, it's likely to show in the next day and a half.' She smiled at him. 'So do I take it that you don't like dogs?'

'No. Just next door's Jack Russell.' Clearly he'd spotted her hospital ID badge, because he groaned. 'Dr Russell. Please don't tell me your first name is Jacqueline.'

She laughed. 'No, it's Emma.'

'Phew!' He fanned himself. 'Don't think I could cope with two Jack Russells in one morning. I'm Mark Bowers, by the way. Pleased to meet you.' Then he rolled his eyes. 'Duh. You already know my name, from my notes.'

'And I'm sure you'd rather not be in here with a hole in your arm,' she said, smiling.

'Ah, but I'm the sort who sees the glass as half full. I might have better things to do with my day off than get bitten by next door's mutt and have to get patched up, but at least I've got someone with a beautiful smile looking after me.'

Rob, writing up notes in the cubicle next door, gritted his teeth. Talk about *cheesy*. Don't say Emma was going to fall for a line like that.

He didn't hear her response, but she'd clearly turned the conversation back to dogs because he heard the patient say, 'I like dogs—just not my neighbour's. What about you?'

'I've got a spaniel,' Emma said.

'King Charles?'

'Springer,' she corrected.

'They're lovely dogs. Completely mad, but lovely natures,' Mark said.

'I wouldn't be without mine.'

That sounded heartfelt. Rob frowned. Was Emma completely on her own? Didn't she have a family? Or was it just that they were living at the other end of the country and she didn't get to see them very often?

'Maybe we could go for a walk together some time,' Mark suggested.

Rob swore under his breath as the cheap ballpoint he was using snapped. This was ridiculous. His relationship with Emma was strictly hospital-based. They were barely even friends, let alone anything else. He really shouldn't be feeling so possessive about her. Especially as he didn't do long-term relationships in any case. He didn't have the right to be jealous.

All the same, when he heard the patient leave the cubicle, he twitched back the curtain between them.

'Can I have a word, Dr Russell?' he asked coolly.

'Sure. Let me just scribble something here…'

The tip of her tongue protruded between her even white teeth as she concentrated on the paperwork, and it made him want to lean forward and nibble her lower lip, to tease her into a kiss.

Then she looked up at him with a half-smile. 'Right, all yours.'

The picture that conjured up set his heart beating just that little bit faster. Oh, no. Not good. He swallowed hard. Keep it professional, he reminded himself. 'I just wanted to remind you that it isn't a good idea to flirt with the patient.'

She frowned. 'Flirt? What do you mean, flirt?'

'You were flirting with the postman—the one with the dog bite.' The one she'd just seen. Surely she couldn't have forgotten that quickly?

Her frown deepened. 'Don't be ridiculous. I wasn't flirting. I was just being friendly.'

He raised an eyebrow. 'That's not what it sounded like.'

'Then maybe you shouldn't eavesdrop.'

He knew he should shut up right now, but his mouth just ran away with him. 'You two were so loud, it wasn't easy to avoid.'

Two spots of colour appeared on her cheeks. And she looked as if she wanted to slap him.

'I just wanted to remind you of the rules.' Ha. Just. More like, he was ragingly jealous that she hadn't said no to the postman, the way she'd refused his own offer of dinner. 'You're not supposed to date patients.'

She rolled her eyes. 'I *know* that. And I don't date patients.'

'He asked you out.'

'Maybe you should've listened a bit harder. I turned him down.'

Oh. He hadn't heard that bit.

And he really shouldn't feel so pleased that she hadn't accepted the date.

'Nicely, I should add, so his feelings weren't hurt and he won't be making a complaint about how horrible the staff are here. And I'd thank you not to interfere in future,' she finished, her voice like ice.

'I'm not interfering,' he protested.

Her face said it all for her. *Much.*

'It's just I know how easily these things happen and I don't want you to end up in a sticky situation.'

She wasn't buying it in the slightest. And no wonder. He wasn't exactly behaving rationally, was he? 'I'm sorry. I just had a friend in London who dated a patient and got into a mess—and I didn't want that to happen to you.' *And I didn't want you to go out with that man. Especially when you could be seeing me.* 'I apologise.'

'Good.'

He glanced at his watch. 'Look, we're due a break. Let me buy you a decent cup of coffee in the canteen to apologise properly.'

'No need. Apology already accepted.'

Though he didn't think it was. Particularly when they were rostered in Resus that afternoon and she kept him at a distance.

The one time his hand accidentally brushed against hers, when they were intubating a patient, made his whole body feel as if it were fizzing. Only years of training kept his mind focused on the patient.

And then it was back to the distance between them. Distance he didn't have a clue how to start bridging. Or why it was even there in the first place.

It was a real relief when the phone rang. 'Keith's bringing in a patient with stomach pains,' he informed her when he'd put down the phone. 'ETA about three minutes.' Theoretically, as her senior, he should lead. But it was obvious she already thought he was overbearing. Time to get some balance back. 'Want to lead on this one?'

'Fine.'

He nodded. 'And I know you're professional enough to say if you need my input, so I'm not going to interfere.'

'Good.'

Keith did the handover when the paramedics arrived. 'Eric Powell, aged forty-nine, severe stomach pains. Started suddenly about half an hour ago. They're worse when he coughs or moves, but no sign of haemorrhage. Sats 98 per cent on oxygen.'

'Thanks, Keith.' Emma smiled at the paramedics. 'Mr Powell? I'm Emma Russell and this is Robert Howarth. We'll be looking after you. I'm going to give you something for the pain, but I need to ask you a couple of questions first. Have you had any pain like this before?'

'No,' Eric croaked.

'Can you show me where the pain is?'

He pointed to his abdomen. So far, inconclusive—she knew that stomach pains were involved in a number of complaints, including respiratory problems, heart disease and problems such as stones in the urinary tract.

'Is it dull or sharp?'

'Sharp. Hurts like hell if I move.'

'And lying still makes it better?'

He nodded.

'Does it hurt anywhere else other than your stomach?'

'Shoulder.'

She quickly went through the rest of the history, establishing that Eric hadn't been sick or had diarrhoea, there were no changes in bowel habits and no history of bleeding, and he'd had no previous surgery. The pain didn't move down to the lower right quadrant of the abdomen, so appendicitis wasn't likely. But Eric had been suffering from indigestion lately—and that definitely rang a bell.

'I've cut back a bit on the late-night curries,' he said, 'but when you're working late it's easier to get a take-away. And I bought some stuff at the chemist that got rid of the indigestion.'

She quickly checked his notes. 'Nothing here about you having an ulcer—do stomach ulcers run in your family at all?'

'Not that I know of. Is that what you think it is—an ulcer?'

'The indigestion makes me think it could be,' she said, 'although I'll need to do some other tests to rule out some other conditions. But first I'm going to give you something for the pain. Sometimes the pain relief makes people feel sick so I'm going to give you something with it to stop that happening, OK?

'A few more questions,' she said. 'Drinking and smoking?'

'Guilty to both,' Eric said ruefully. 'They help me relax.'

'They also make you more likely to have a stomach ulcer,' she said gently.

His pulse and respirations were reasonably normal, and his temperature was up slightly. Caused by an infection? Or was it something else?

'I'm going to ask you for a urine sample,' she said, 'and do some blood tests.' She turned to Rob. 'I'm also going to do an ultrasound and a chest X-ray because they tend to be more useful at this stage than abdominal films.'

'Any thoughts on a diagnosis?' Rob asked.

Definitely. 'I'm thinking a perforated peptic ulcer.'

'There's no evidence of a GI bleed,' Rob reminded her. 'And Mr Powell doesn't have a history of a peptic ulcer.'

'It could have perforated before it's been diagnosed,' Emma said. 'Mr Powell's indigestion could be due to his lifestyle—long working hours and the kind of diet that usually goes with it—but it's also one of the first symptoms of an ulcer. His stomach pain is localised epigastric pain that's spread to the abdomen and the shoulder tip.'

'Which is common with a peptic ulcer,' Robert agreed. 'OK. Order the tests.'

The chest X-rays showed free gas under the diaphragm. The ultrasound didn't show anything out of the ordinary, but when Emma glanced at the blood tests, she nodded and then looked straight at Robert. 'I'd say this is pretty conclusive. His white cell count's up and so is the amylase. That, plus the free gas—which you find in about three-quarters of patients with perforated ulcers—makes me pretty sure that's what this is.'

He smiled. 'Good call. And your next move?'

'Give him prophylactic antibiotics and refer him to the surgical team. I'll explain to Mr Powell what a peptic ulcer is and what the surgeon's going to do.'

'Excellent.' Robert spread his hands. 'All yours, Dr Russell.'

They walked back over to their patient. 'Mr Powell, I'm pretty sure you have a peptic ulcer. It's where there's a raw patch in the lining of your stomach—under a gastroscope it would look pretty much like a mouth ulcer,' Emma explained. 'The contents of your stomach are acidic, to break down your food and protect you from infection, but if your stomach produces too much acid or there isn't enough mucus in the lining of your stomach, you end up with an ulcer. The pain usually feels like indigestion. Do you find that yours is worse just after you've had something to eat?'

'Yes. I thought it was just because I eat a bit late.' Eric pulled a face. 'I mean, I'm not going to bother my GP with a bit of indigestion when I can get something at the supermarket for it.'

'Thing is,' Emma said, 'if you'd seen your GP about it, your ulcer could've been diagnosed before it perforated—right now, you're going to need surgery to repair the hole in the ulcer.'

'I need an operation?' He looked shocked.

'The good news is, you won't have to have a general anaesthetic. I'll get the surgeon to come and see you and explain it fully, but basically you'll be sedated and a flexible tube will go down your throat so the surgeon can see what's happening in your stomach and do the repair. And the treatment after that depends on whether you have a certain bacterium in your stomach—you might be given antibiotics and you'll probably be given some acid-reducing medicine.' She smiled. 'And there are some things you can do yourself to help. Spicy foods are one of the things that make ulcers worse—as do smoking and alcohol. And would I be right in guessing that you normally have a cup of coffee on the go at work?'

'Guilty,' he said ruefully.

'I'm not saying give it all up completely,' she said, 'just that you'll find they make the pain from the ulcer worse. Same as you'll need to be careful what you take for a headache in future—it's a good idea to avoid ibuprofen and aspirin, as they tend to be a bit too harsh on your stomach.'

'Paracetamol doesn't touch my headaches, though,' Eric said.

'Then you need to see your GP and get something a bit stronger that'll work on the headache but still be gentle on your stomach,' Emma said.

'An ulcer.' He shook his head. 'My wife's always saying I work too hard and I'd end up with an ulcer.'

'Stress makes your stomach produce more acid,' Emma said, 'so although it doesn't strictly cause an ulcer, it can make the symptoms of an ulcer worse. So I reckon you've got a good reason to take things a bit easier.' She smiled at him. 'Has anyone at work called your wife, or would you like us to call her and tell her you're here?'

'They were supposed to have called her at work when I collapsed,' he said.

He didn't sound that convinced that his colleagues had done so—and the last thing she wanted was her patient worrying. 'Give me the number, and I'll call her just in case,' Emma said. 'Plus I can give her an update so she won't have to worry so much.'

'Thanks, love.' Eric squeezed her hand. 'And bless you for guessing she'd worry. Or do all daughters know what their mums are like?'

'Something like that.'

Her tone was still light but Rob saw the flash of bleakness in Emma's eyes. It was gone so quickly he wasn't a hundred per cent sure it had been there at all. But it made him wonder: what made Emma Russell tick? And was he right in his earlier guess that she didn't have a family?

When Emma had called Mrs Powell and Eric was with the surgeons, Rob said to her, 'You were very good with him. Even though he was doing all the wrong things for an ulcer, lifestyle-wise, you didn't nag him.'

She shrugged. 'I don't nag. It doesn't work. It just puts people on the defensive.'

And right now she was definitely on the defensive with him.

Finally it was their last case of the day—a traffic accident where airbags had been deployed, so the driver and passenger had been brought in to be checked for possible spinal injuries. Luckily it turned out to be nothing more serious than bruising, but this time Rob took the lead, talking Emma through what he was doing and asking her the odd difficult question—and she clearly enjoyed having all the answers.

If only he could get past this physical thing, Rob thought, he'd have a ball, working with Emma. She was a good doctor, thorough in her assessments and great with people. He liked her.

The problem was, his feelings for her weren't just professional.

He had to find a way of settling into a decent working relationship with her.

But he had a nasty feeling that the only way that would happen was if they had some kind of mad affair to get it out of his system. Given the way she'd reacted to him so far, he was pretty sure she'd rebuff him if he suggested it.

Though if this went on for much longer, he might be driven crazy enough to try it.

CHAPTER FOUR

THAT evening, Rob drove over to the village hall where the Fellside search and rescue team were based. He'd called them earlier in the week to see if he could join them, bearing in mind that he was an experienced climber as well as a qualified emergency doctor. And his timing had been lucky because they'd just been let down by the anaesthetist who'd promised to give them a talk on drugs for their training night that evening. Ken, the search and rescue team leader, was delighted at Rob's offer to stand in and promised to discuss joining the team then.

When Rob walked into the room and saw Emma in the front row, he stared at her in surprise.

A surprise she clearly shared, because her expression mirrored exactly what he was thinking: *What on earth are* you *doing here?*

It was pretty obvious why he was here—he was doing the training evening. But she'd told him she didn't climb—so why would she be at a training evening for the local search and rescue team? It didn't make sense.

There was a dog curled at her feet, he noticed. The springer spaniel he'd heard her mention to her patient that morning. A beautiful dog with a glossy brown-and-white coat, clearly very used to the surrounding group of people and completely unperturbed by the chatter going on.

Ken introduced him to the couple of dozen people sitting in the village hall. 'This is Dr Robert Howarth, who's agreed to step in at short notice and cover our training session on medication,' Ken said.

'Thank you very much for asking me along. I'm delighted to be here,' Rob said. 'I've spent the last few years working in London, but I've climbed for years and years—so I'm looking forward to exploring the area around here, though I sincerely hope I won't see any of you except on a social basis.'

There was a murmur of polite laughter.

So far, so expected.

'I'm a registrar in the emergency department at Fellside Hospital—in fact, I work with Emma Russell, whom you all obviously know.'

He glanced at her and noted the slight bloom of colour in her cheeks. Well, what else was he meant to do? Ignore her? Pretend they didn't work together?

'So, medication in the mountain rescue kit. We'll start with pain relief—Entonox. It's usually used for labour pains, but it can be pretty effective for lower limb injuries. Are any of you sitting the mountain rescue casualty care exams in the spring?'

A murmur of surprise: clearly nobody here expected him to know they existed, let alone when they were. Good, he thought. With any luck it'd make them take him more seriously.

One or two people stuck their hands up in answer to his question. He smiled. 'You'll probably get a question on Entonox in the exam. So can anyone here tell me what it is?'

Silence.

He was pretty sure it wasn't because nobody knew what it was—more like nobody wanted to be the first one to answer. Much as he hated to do this, there were only two people he knew here tonight: Ken and Emma. And Emma was an absolute definite for knowing the answer.

'Sorry to pick on you, Dr Russell. Would you mind?'

Her expression called him a liar—that he wasn't sorry in the slightest—but she nodded. 'Nitrous oxide and oxygen.'

'Thank you. And what's the temperature threshold for administering it to a casualty?'

'Zero degrees,' someone called back.

'Excellent. Theoretically speaking, you could go a couple of degrees below but it's safest to stick to policy. When it gets to minus six degrees, the nitrous oxide turns into a liquid and separates from the oxygen, so it's completely useless as pain relief. Anyone know why?'

Still no response.

He cast Emma a pleading look.

Would she bail him out this time, too?

She sighed. 'Because the patient would breathe in pure oxygen from the first half of the cylinder—it would help with their breathing but do absolutely nothing for pain relief.'

'Exactly. And when the oxygen is depleted and the pressure in the cylinder lowers, the nitrous oxide turns back into a gas—which could be fatal if our patient breathes it in.'

Luckily it got livelier when he moved on to the other drugs carried in the mountain rescue team's medical kit—stronger pain relief, medication for asthma and allergic reactions, and the medication used for cardiovascular emergencies. He was about to move on to IV access and fluids when Ken's mobile phone went.

'Callout,' Ken said. 'Man in his fifties, walking on his own, should've been back three hours ago and his wife's called him in missing. Good news is that he told her where he was planning to walk, so we can narrow it down a bit. Sorry, Rob, we're going to have to stop you there.'

'No worries. I can come back another time.'

'It's not the first time we've had to do a training session in two bits because of a callout,' Ken said ruefully.

Rob followed Ken over to the room where the team clearly kept their equipment. 'I've got my climbing gear in the boot of my car. Do you need an extra body for the search?'

Ken looked at him. 'It's nice of you to offer, but—'

'I'm not a qualified team member and I don't know the area,' Rob finished wryly. 'I know we were going to discuss it tonight and we don't have time to go through it properly now. But I've been climbing for years. I've done the Three Peaks challenge four times, so I know I've got the stamina and the ability you need. Plus I'm a qualified emergency doctor.'

Ken frowned. 'Well, you could be with us as a probationer for tonight. Though you'll need to stick with one of the others—and no heroics,' he warned.

'The casualty's the important one here, so that means teamwork, not solo showing off,' Rob said. '"No heroics" is fine by me.'

'Good. And as you already know Emma, it makes sense for you to work with her—if she's OK with that.' Ken called her over. 'Em—can you do us a favour, love?'

She smiled at him. 'Sure.'

'Can you work with Rob here?'

She blinked. 'What?'

'Can you work with Rob?' Ken repeated. 'He says he's an experienced climber.'

She stared at Rob. 'You've spent the past four years working in London—unless I'm in some weird parallel universe, there aren't any mountains in London or any mountain rescue teams there either.'

'No, but I spent my time off climbing. And I'm a trained doctor. And I'm planning to stay at Fellside for a few years so

I may as well start as I mean to go on and join the team now—I want to put something back into the community. I'll do proper training as and when, but for now I'm here to help out and, as a probationer, I'm under your direction this evening.'

'Good. That's sorted, then,' Ken said, clapping them both on the back.

'I don't believe this,' Emma muttered, out of Ken's hearing.

'Think of it this way: it puts things in balance. I'm your senior at the hospital, and you're my senior here,' Rob said.

She shook her head. 'This is a nightmare.'

'What's so hard about working with me?'

She didn't answer.

Wouldn't or couldn't? Rob wondered.

They didn't have time to hang about and discuss it now: they had a job to do. Maybe she wasn't ready to resolve whatever the problem was between them, but he needed to push the boundaries just enough to make this workable. 'All right. I'll ask you a question. Do you trust me as a doctor?' he asked softly.

She looked at him directly, her green eyes very clear. 'Yes.'

'Then believe me when I tell you I'm as dedicated to climbing as I am to medicine. I'm not a complete rookie who'll need you to get him out of trouble and I'm not going to let you down, Emma.' He paused. 'Though I could point out that you lied to me. You said you don't climb for fun.'

'I don't.'

He didn't get it. 'Then why are you here with the rescue team?'

She shrugged. 'Byron's my dog. And he's a trained SARDA dog.'

With the amount of time it took to train a SARDA dog—and given that less than half of rescue dogs who started training ended up being graded for the callout lists—Emma was definitely serious about being part of the rescue team. Yet she didn't climb for fun. Something didn't quite add up. 'What happened? Did you lose someone?' he asked.

'Not to climbing.' Then she clapped a hand to her mouth, looking shocked, as if she'd told him something she hadn't intended to share.

He took her other hand and squeezed it briefly. 'I think maybe we need to talk. Later. But right now we have work to do. And, as I'm working with you, I'd better introduce myself to your partner.' He squatted down and held his hand out for the dog to sniff. When the spaniel nudged his hand in acceptance, he smiled and stroked the top of the dog's head. 'Hello—aren't you beautiful?' He looked up at Emma. 'What's her name?'

'*His* name's Byron.'

'Mad, bad and dangerous to know?'

She smiled back. 'Lucy named him after her favourite poet—but, no, not in this case. Byron's the sweetest-tempered springer I've ever met.'

He could well believe it. The dog was handsome, with a brown face and a tiny splash of white on his nose, and his big brown eyes were soulful. 'Hello, Byron. I'm Rob.'

The spaniel licked him. Rob smiled, fussed the dog a bit more and stood up. 'Who's Lucy?' he asked, deliberately keeping his voice casual.

'My sister.' Emma's eyes glittered and Rob knew there was something she wasn't telling him. Maybe Lucy was the reason why Emma did SARDA work. He'd get her to tell him later.

Ken briefed the team rapidly and gave them all an area to cover, reminding them that they would be taking the 'wall of light and sound' approach. 'You said you had climbing gear, Rob. Does that include a whistle and a torch?'

'And spare batteries,' Rob confirmed. 'I've got a small medical kit with me and a space blanket. And my rucksack's got enough room for splints.'

'We've got a lightweight stretcher, too,' Ken said. 'Can you and Emma take half each?'

'Sure.' Rob turned to Emma. 'Are we taking my car or yours?'

'Byron and I walked here,' she said.

'OK. You navigate, I'll drive,' he said.

She coughed. 'And Byron?'

He smiled. 'He'll be just fine in the back of my car. I'm not bothered by a bit of mud.'

As Emma had half suspected, Rob had a four-wheel-drive car and there was plenty of room in the back for her rucksack and the stretcher, as well as for Byron.

'Before you say it, no, this isn't a "Chelsea tractor",' he said. 'Although I worked in London, as I told you, I spent a lot of my free time climbing. Which meant I needed a car that wasn't fussy about potholes in car parks.'

'And it'll be useful here in winter—the roads can be a bit grim,' she admitted.

'Feel free to fiddle with the stereo,' he said, climbing into the driver's seat.

Stereo wasn't quite the description she'd have used. State-of-the-art sound system was more like it. She flicked through the play lists and discovered Rob's tastes were pretty much as she'd expected: contemporary indie rock. The kind of stuff she listened to, too. She picked a play list she liked the sound of and he gave her a sidelong look.

'Good choice. This is one of the best sets I know to drive to. Now—you know the area so I'm completely in your hands. Directions?' he asked.

Emma directed him to the area they'd been assigned. Rob parked safely, then they changed into walking boots, put on their waterproofs and started to walk through the area. 'We're doing what's known as a wall of light and sound,' she told him.

'It's one of the best ways of communicating with the team and with a conscious casualty at night. The idea is that we stop at regular intervals and use our torches and whistles in an agreed pattern. Hopefully the casualty will hear us and will make a noise so we can find them. Or if the casualty's unconscious, the idea is that Byron will find him and stay there, barking to lead us to him.'

'What kind of injuries do you get most out here?' Rob asked.

'Lower leg—though there's often mild hypothermia. It's not too cold tonight, but even so, if you're injured and you've been stuck in one place, you'll lose body heat. Especially if water's been involved.'

'Point taken,' Rob said. 'Do you have any warming devices?'

'Dry clothes and your space blanket. Though we were thinking about trialling one of those little portable machines.'

They walked along in silence for a while. Then he asked, 'Have you had Byron long?'

'He's three. I've had him since he was eight weeks old,' she said.

'So you've worked on the rescue team for, what? Three years?'

'Four years. Just after I qualified as a doctor,' she said. 'Though obviously two years of those were spent training Byron.'

Which was a long, long time for someone who didn't like climbing. What made her do this? Rob wondered again.

They kept searching—the dog alternately racing off and coming back. Eventually Byron didn't come back, and they heard barking. Emma radioed through to the rest of the team and there was silence. 'Hello?' she yelled.

There was a faint answering cry, and Byron barked again.

'Sounds as if it's coming from over there,' Rob said. 'You know the area better than I do. Anything I need to look out for?'

'The ground's a bit rough, so watch your footing,' Emma said. 'Cheers.'

Finally they reached the casualty—who, to their relief, was conscious and with no sign of confusion. Clearly there wasn't a head injury involved.

Emma dropped to her haunches by the dog and rewarded him. 'Well done, boy,' she said softly. 'You found him.' She turned to the casualty. 'Mr Fisher, I presume?'

'Yes. Am I glad to see you,' he said feelingly. 'I thought I was going to be stuck out here all night. The battery on my mobile's flat so I couldn't call for help.'

'Luckily you'd told your wife when to expect you back and which path you were taking,' Emma said, 'so she told us you were missing and roughly where you'd be. I'm Emma and this is Rob. How are you feeling?'

'Stiff and cold.'

'What happened?' she asked.

He looked embarrassed. 'I should know better at my age. I was taking a photo and not looking where I was going. I slipped. I think I've broken my ankle—I definitely can't stand and it hurts even to crawl if I drag my leg.'

'You're in good hands,' Rob told him. 'We're both doctors in the emergency department at Fellside General.'

Emma radioed through to Ken to let him know they'd found their casualty. Meanwhile Rob examined Mr Fisher's ankle. 'Yep, definitely broken,' he said. He put a splint on it. 'Stretcher job,' he said to Emma, and helped her put the two halves of the lightweight stretcher together.

By the time they'd helped Mr Fisher out of his damp fleece and put a space blanket round him and a dry hat on his head, the rest of the team were there to help carry him to the road, where the ambulance met them and whisked him off to Fellside General.

'Good work, team,' Ken said. 'Enjoy your first rescue, Rob?'

'Yeah. Because my partner and her dog were excellent,' he said.

'Hmm,' was Emma's only comment.

'It's a bit too late now to finish off the talk,' Ken said. 'Can you come back next week, Rob?'

'Sure.'

'Good. See you all next week. Callouts permitting, of course.'

Emma and Rob returned to the car; when he opened the boot to let the dog in, he made a fuss of the spaniel.

To Emma's disgust, the admiration was entirely mutual. Byron, out of work mode, rolled onto his back and flopped a paw in Rob's direction, demanding a tummy rub.

'Dogs are normally good judges of character,' Rob said thoughtfully. 'Your dog likes me—so why don't you?'

The question threw her off balance. 'I didn't say I didn't like you.'

'Actions speak louder than words. It's in the way you look at me,' he said softly. 'And you avoid me as much as you can.'

Yeah. Because Robert Howarth was a beautiful man—and she'd learned the hard way about getting involved with beautiful men.

'So what's the problem?' Rob asked.

'You're a party animal,' she said.

'So you think I'm shallow?'

She flushed. 'That's not what I said.'

'It's what your face is saying. Why don't you get to know me better and see if there's something more beneath the surface?'

'Because maybe there isn't.'

He laughed. 'I like you, Emma. And I think you'd be good for me.'

She made a noise of disgust. 'I'm not going to be your therapy.'

'Believe me, therapy's not what I have in mind.'

His voice was husky and sexy and put the most X-rated pictures into her head. 'So what *did* you have in mind?' she asked, before she could stop the words coming out.

He leaned against the car's bumper. 'Whether you like it or not, Emma, there's something between us.'

She didn't have a chance to make a retort, because he reached out, yanked her into his arms and brushed his mouth against hers.

It felt as if the sky was lit up by a shower of meteors. Brilliant, blinding light searing across the darkness of the universe. And when he caught her lower lip between his, nibbling gently, she was helpless to resist. She let him deepen the kiss, touching the tip of her tongue against his and sliding her arms round his neck. He'd widened his stance slightly so she was cradled between his thighs.

And it felt like coming home.

A nudge against her side from the dog brought her back to her senses, and she pulled away. What *had* she been thinking? And how long had they been kissing like that? Her whole body was tingling, and if she hadn't been wearing a thick sweater the erect state of her nipples would've been very obvious.

'That wasn't supposed to happen,' she said shakily.

'But it did.' His face was completely unreadable. 'What do you suggest we do about it?'

She swallowed hard. 'Absolutely nothing.'

'We could try. But I knew from the minute I first met you that it was going to happen. And don't lie—you felt it, too.'

When they'd shaken hands. And every single nerve-end had gone up in flames. 'Yeah,' she admitted.

'It's going to happen again,' Rob said softly. 'And I don't think we're going to be able to stop it.'

She had a nasty feeling that he was right. 'So what do you suggest we do, then?'

'Have a mad affair. Get it out of our systems—and then we can go back to normal.'

For a moment she was tempted. Seriously tempted. The

way he'd kissed her had sent her knees weak; she knew that making love with Rob would be incredible. Beyond her wildest dreams.

But then common sense kicked back in. 'No, that's not a good idea. Rob, I don't want to get involved with anyone.'

'Been burned?' he asked softly.

Was it that obvious? No point in lying about it. She nodded.

'So what are you going to do about it? Live like a nun and then when you're ninety realise you've let him ruin your whole life because you wouldn't give anyone else a chance?'

Her eyes narrowed. 'Is that why you date women twice and then drop them?'

He frowned. 'How do you mean?'

'Never underestimate the hospital grapevine. You have a reputation as a love-'em-and-leave-'em man.'

'Actually, I do mutual relationships,' he corrected.

'Just not long ones.'

'OK, not long ones,' he admitted wryly.

'Maximum two dates,' she pointed out.

He raked a hand through his hair. 'Look, I never lie to anyone I've been involved with. They know I'm not in it for the long term. We have fun while it lasts. And if the grapevine's reported accurately, you'll also know I've remained on friendly terms with all my exes. I'm not a complete louse.'

'So when *you're* ninety you'll realise you've let her ruin your whole life because you won't let anyone else get close to you?' She threw his words back at him.

'Touché.' He reached out and traced the curve of her jaw with a fingertip. 'So maybe, Emma Russell, we're both as bad as each other.'

'Maybe.'

'So maybe,' he added softly, 'we might be good for each other—we might even be able to help each other.' He let his hand slide back to the nape of her neck and gently removed the scrunchie from her hair, so it fell about her face.

She stared at him. 'Why did you do that?'

'Because I wanted to see what you look like with your hair down.' He dragged in a breath. 'I apologise. I really shouldn't have done that.'

Her mouth felt as if she'd eaten a whole desertful of sand. 'Why not?'

'You know why not.'

She shook her head. 'I'm not a mind-reader.'

'You're not going to like this,' he warned.

'Try me.'

He took a deep breath. 'Because it's made me want to see your hair spread over my pillow.'

She groaned. 'Do you use lines like that on every woman who attracts your attention? That's *incredibly* corny.'

'And incredibly true. Just for the record, I don't.' He gave her a wry smile. 'I'm usually suave and sophisticated.'

The self-mockery was evident—and she found it appealing. Dangerously so.

'With you, my mouth runs away with me before my brain clicks into gear. I know there are all sorts of reasons why we shouldn't get together. Everything from the fact that we work together through to the fact you've been hurt in the past and so have I. With my head, I know we should keep things as they are. But the rest of me's not listening to my head. At all.' He twirled the end of her hair round his finger. 'Your hair's so soft. I want to touch you, Em. Explore you slowly. Until we're both in flames.'

She gave the tiniest shake of her head. 'I don't do relationships.'

'Neither do I.'

'I'm not the sort for flings either.'

'I know.' He sighed. 'That doesn't change the fact that there's something there between us.'

'Yeah, yeah.'

'Em. We work well together at the hospital. We worked well together tonight. And I think we'd be very…' he leaned forward and brushed his mouth against hers '…*very* good together.' He rubbed the pad of his thumb against her lower lip. 'You know, it's going to happen,' he said, his voice a husky, sexy whisper.

'In your dreams.'

He gave her a slow, sultry smile. 'Too late. That's *already* happened.'

Emma felt colour shoot into her face. He'd dreamed about her, the way she'd dreamed about him? X-rated dreams?

'And I think,' he added softly, 'that the reality is going to be even better than the dream.' He brushed his mouth against hers again, and her whole body tingled. 'But for now I'm going to drop you home. I'm not going to expect you to ask me in.' He gave her a faint smile. 'If you did, I'd say yes and we'd both be late for work tomorrow. Despite the fact we're on a late shift.'

She felt her eyes widen. 'You've got a high opinion of your irresistibility.'

'No, I'm being honest. This is mutual. I wouldn't be able to resist you either. One thing would lead to another—very, very quickly. Neither of us would have the slightest control over it. Neither of us would be able to say "stop".' He stole another kiss. 'So what I'm going to do when I've driven you home is sit in the car and wait until you and Byron are safely indoors. And then I'm going back to my place for a long cold shower.'

She had a feeling she'd need one of those, too.

'And tomorrow,' he said, 'tomorrow—we're going to talk. Properly.'

CHAPTER FIVE

THERE was no time to talk at work on Friday afternoon because the emergency department was particularly busy and Rob and Emma were both rostered in Resus, right in the thick of things.

'Emma, I need you with me for this one,' Rob said when he put the phone down in the middle of the afternoon. 'ETA three minutes. Motorcyclist who was in a head-on collision and thrown onto the central reservation. They've got him in a collar on a spinal board, but my guess is we might be dealing with multiple fractures. And we'd better hope it's not a type C pelvic fracture.'

Emma knew exactly what he meant—a type C pelvic fracture meant that the pelvic ring had snapped in at least two places, so it was unstable both rotationally and vertically. It usually involved soft-tissue injuries and massive blood loss, leading to hypovolaemic shock or even death. 'Fingers crossed,' she said.

The second that Kevin had finished the handover, Rob and Emma set to work checking the patient's airway and circulation. Rob put two large cannulae in the motorcyclist's forearm and Emma gently put the patient onto high-flow oxygen and gave him pain relief, explaining to Colin Faraday what she was doing as she did it and reassuring him that they were going to be able to help him.

'I'm not happy with Colin's blood pressure,' Rob said quietly to Emma. 'And he's pale and clammy.'

Colin had admitted to feeling light-headed. It could be from pain—but it could also be from an internal bleed.

'I've got a gut feeling about this,' Rob said. 'Kirsty, please, can you organise a pelvic X-ray plus both legs? And I'd like eight units of blood cross-matched too, please.'

'Are you thinking pelvic fracture?' Emma asked.

Rob nodded. 'I'm not sure how bad—we'll need an X-ray to tell us that. And from the look of the swelling in his right thigh, I think we're looking at long-bone injuries as well. We need to be careful with a clinical exam here, as we can cause even more damage to the soft tissues.'

Gently, he examined Colin for soft-tissue injuries.

'Are you going to do a DPL?' Emma asked. Diagnostic peritoneal lavage was a good way of checking for internal injuries.

'Not this time. We could make things worse if the injuries are really severe—and when you think of the force needed to crack a pelvic bone… It's too much of a risk. I'm sending him for a CT scan.'

The X-ray results were back first. Rob sat Emma in front of the computer screen. 'What can you see on this X-ray?' he asked.

'Broken femur, obviously. I'd say it's a transfer fracture, caused by the transfer of energy in the accident.'

'Can you describe it for me?'

'Fifty per cent displacement, but there's no angulation or shortening. Lucky it's a clean break—to be honest, I was expecting it to be comminuted. Shattered into little pieces. Obviously I can't tell from the X-ray alone if the fracture is open or closed, but the clinical examination earlier tells me it's closed because there's bruising on his leg but no sign of the bone protruding.'

'How would you expect the orthopods to deal with it?' Rob asked.

'On its own, I'd say with a functional brace, so the cast keeps the fracture aligned properly but the patient's able to move his knee and put weight on it. But with that pelvic fracture as well—' a fracture Rob had shown her in one of the other X-rays and which to their relief was a single, stable fracture '—I don't know.'

'Could be external fixator, could be internal. I'm not going to second-guess the orthopods here,' Rob said. 'We'll splint for now.'

They both walked over to Colin.

'How are you feeling?' Emma asked gently, taking his hand.

'Pretty rough,' he admitted. 'So what've I done?'

'Broken your right thigh and your pelvis. You're lucky, though,' Rob said.

'Lucky? With two breaks?' Colin looked disbelievingly at him.

'It wasn't your spine or your neck,' Rob said. 'Could've been a hell of a lot worse.'

'So how long am I going to be in hospital?'

'I'm waiting for your CT scan results—you'll be in Theatre today to get those breaks sorted, and if you've got internal injuries as well the surgical team will sort those out, too,' Rob said. 'And then you'll be in for a few days for observation—we'll want to keep an eye on you in case any infection develops.'

'And until I can walk again?'

'Depends on what the surgeons do. It takes up to two months for fractures in your arm and four months for fractures in your leg to heal,' Rob said, 'and that's provided there aren't any complications. But the physios will want to get you up on your feet again as soon as possible to stop your muscles wasting too much. Could be quite a few months before you get your movement back to the full range, though, depending on how quickly your pelvis heals.' He smiled wryly. 'Sorry I can't give you anything more definite. The othopods will be able to tell you more when you come out of Theatre.'

Colin sighed. 'My girlfriend hates my motorbike. She'll never allow me near one again after this.'

'She might come round if she realises how much it means to you,' Rob said. 'Then again—she might not.'

Something in his tone alerted Emma. Was this why Rob didn't do relationships? He'd had a motorcycle accident and his girlfriend had decided she couldn't handle the risks any more? Although, working in London, he'd probably dealt with more than the average number of traffic accidents, this sounded like personal experience rather than something to do with work.

She waited until they were on their break before asking him.

'Coffee,' she said, handing him a mug.

'Cheers.' Rob tipped the first inch out of the mug, replacing it with cold water, and drank it straight down.

'In need of a caffeine hit?' she asked.

'Something like that.'

She took a sip of her own drink. 'So when did you smash up your motorbike, then?'

He shook his head. 'Never had one.'

'The way you were talking to Colin Faraday, it sounded like you'd been through the same thing.'

He shrugged. 'Maybe.'

She rolled her eyes. 'This is like pulling teeth. What did you do? Pelvic fracture?'

'Nope.'

When she put down the mug, folded her arms and looked at him, he sighed. 'All right. I smashed both legs and both arms. At one point they thought my spine might be involved as well.'

She blinked. 'Hell's bells. That's a lot of fractures, Rob.'

'Yeah. You know the cartoons where they have a bloke in traction, with both legs and arms in full casts and a bandage around his head?' He gave her a self-deprecating smile. 'That was me—well, without the head bandage. And I watched more mind-numbing TV in the months I was stuck in bed than I had in my whole life put together before that. I must have driven the nurses mad, begging them for audio books or anything to keep my mind off how bored I was—I couldn't even hold a pen to do a crossword or anything, at one point.'

She raised an eyebrow. 'Most people can manage to write with a broken arm.'

'Yeah. Except I broke my thumb and middle finger as well—on my right hand.'

His writing hand. And if he'd ever been planning a career in surgery, his operating hand. So that accident could've been life-changing in more than one way. 'Ouch.' She sucked in a breath. 'You said it wasn't a motorcycle accident. I'm not sure I dare ask how you did that much damage.'

'Climbing,' he said cheerfully. 'Fell off a mountain about five years ago.'

She blinked. 'Hang on. You were in plaster for months, physio for even longer—and you *still* climb for fun?'

'Yup.' He smiled at her. 'There's nothing like it. The feeling of being on top of the world. And I'm a hell of a lot more safety-conscious nowadays. So, before you start panicking and get on the phone to Ken, let me reassure you that I'm not going to be a liability to the mountain rescue team. I don't put people at risk. *Ever.*'

He'd been in plaster for weeks. And he hadn't mentioned anything about visitors. 'So if you were that bored, I take it you were in a hospital too far away for your family to visit you much?'

'They did their bit.'

There was a definite 'but' there—something he wasn't telling her. 'But?' she asked softly.

'Nothing. I just have a low boredom threshold.'

That was one way of accounting for his 'two dates and

you're out' reputation. But she knew there was something more to it than that. He'd as good as admitted it after their rescue. 'What was her name?'

He sighed. 'All right. Her name was Natasha.'

She waited, knowing that if she left it he was more likely to fill the silence.

'I can see why she was mad at me—the accident was a month before we were supposed to get married, and I guess having me in a wheelchair with four limbs in plaster wouldn't have looked too good in the wedding photos.'

Now, that she *hadn't* expected. Robert Howarth had been engaged? How come the hospital grapevine hadn't reported that? She tried to hide her surprise. 'Couldn't you have moved the wedding back a bit? Until you were out of plaster?'

He shrugged again. 'Didn't work out that way.'

So who had ended it? Rob or Natasha?

'And I guess when you're twenty-five with your whole life ahead of you, you don't want to be tied to a cripple.'

Natasha, then. She flinched. That was way too close to home. Almost exactly the same words she'd heard before— about someone she'd loved very, very much. 'You're much better off without her.'

'Now, *that* sounds heartfelt.' His gaze met hers. 'I told you. Are you going to tell me?'

She shook her head. 'Not here.'

'Ah. So it's not the telling you object to. It's the place.'

'You're twisting my words.'

'Let's put it another way. I answered your questions. Are you going to answer mine?'

'Not right now.'

'So it's not the time or the place?' His gaze seemed to be firmly fixed on her mouth, and she shivered, remembering the way he'd kissed her the previous night. A kiss that had seriously interfered with her sleep, despite her cool shower. 'OK. So we need somewhere quiet. Somewhere we won't be interrupted or overheard. Somewhere we'll be alone.'

She dragged in a breath. He wasn't talking about finding them a place to make love. She really ought to get her mind out of the gutter.

'Have dinner with me tonight. You know the area—you tell me where's a good place. Somewhere little and quiet where we can talk.'

'I—'

She didn't get the chance to answer, because Kirsty popped her head round the door. 'Em, sorry, I know you're on a break but I've got a case where I really need you.'

Rob raised an eyebrow. 'Emma specifically?'

'Yes.' The nurse was very definite. 'Sorry to mess up your break.'

'That's fine,' Emma said, pouring her coffee into the sink and rinsing out her mug.

'Busy out there?' Rob asked.

Kirsty nodded. 'Typical Friday afternoon.'

Rob rinsed out his mug. 'I'm due in cubicles so I might as well come through now, too. Catch you later, Em.'

His tone was casual, but she knew he meant it. He wasn't going to let her off the hook. She was going to have to tell him.

The second she glanced at the notes Kirsty gave her, she knew exactly why the nurse had requested her.

Because the case involved something she knew more about than anyone else in the department, including the senior consultant.

Motor neurone disease.

The disease that had killed her sister. The disease that still cast a shadow over her own future.

Even though it felt as if someone was ripping off the top

layer of her scars, this was her job. And she'd do it to the very best of her ability.

She walked into the cubicle and smiled at the woman lying on the bed. 'Hello, Mrs Rivers. I'm Emma Russell. Don't try to talk right now, because I know it's a real effort and you can do without the extra strain. Let's get your breathing sorted out first. Kirsty's a star because she's already put you on oxygen and that's going to help. But I want to change your position just very slightly here to make things a bit easier for you. If that's OK, can you move your right hand?'

The woman looked at her in surprise, followed by relief, then moved her right hand.

'Great.' Gently, she moved Mrs Rivers to an easier position.

'I see you've just moved to the area, so I don't have all your notes to hand and don't know your medical history in as much detail as I'd like. I'm going to ask you some questions, but I'll do them so you can sign the answers instead of struggling to answer. So move your right hand for yes and your left for no.'

A tear rolled down the woman's cheek, and she removed the mask. 'You're…first…understand,' she rasped.

'I understand.' Emma gently brushed the tear away. 'That's why Kirsty called me in particular to help you. Has your family been called yet?'

Mrs Rivers spread her palms.

'Not sure?' Emma guessed.

Mrs Rivers moved her right hand.

Emma nodded. 'Then we'll call them to be on the safe side. Would it be easier for you to write the number than say it?'

Mrs Rivers moved her right hand.

'OK.' Emma took a pen from the pocket of her white coat and handed it and her clipboard to Mrs Rivers, who wrote down a number and a name. The writing was slightly shaky but legible.

'Your husband?' Emma guessed.

Mrs Rivers moved her right hand.

'I'll get our receptionist to call him. Back in a second.' She left the cubicle and made her way swiftly to reception.

'Ruth, can you make a call for me, please?' She handed the receptionist the piece of paper. 'This is the patient's husband. Mrs Rivers. Can you tell him she's been brought in here and we're making her comfortable?'

'Sure. I'll do it now.'

'Thanks.'

Ruth picked up the phone, and Emma returned to cubicles. 'We're getting in touch with your husband, Mrs Rivers. Now, I'm going to listen to your chest. It's my guess that you've got a chest infection and that's what's causing your breathing problems right now. Would I be right in saying you're finding it harder to swallow nowadays?'

Mrs Rivers moved her right hand.

Ah, hell. In the late stages of motor neurone disease, breathing and swallowing were difficult. Which meant the patient became more prone to chest infections, and their immune system was lower, too, because they weren't eating properly—and the chest infection made it even harder to breathe and swallow. It was a vicious circle that got tighter and tighter.

'How long ago was your MND diagnosed?' she asked. 'Can you hold up fingers for years first?'

Three years.

'Months?'

Eight.

Almost exactly the same as Lucy's when…

She swallowed hard. OK. She was a doctor. This was her job. She could put her emotions aside. Block them off. Concentrate on her patient, not let it get personal.

She made a note, then said, 'I'm going to listen to your

chest now.' She placed the end of the stethoscope on Mrs Rivers's chest. 'Can you breathe in for me? And out? That's great.' She moved the stethoscope. 'And again? Thank you.' She took the earpieces out. 'I'm not going to make you move so I can listen to your back—I already know what I'm going to hear. You've definitely got a chest infection, so I'm going to put you on antibiotics to clear it up. But I also want to refer you to the neuro team today to see if they can make you a bit more comfortable. Do you want me to get you some water?'

Mrs Rivers moved her right hand. 'Please,' she rasped behind the oxygen mask.

'Is a straw easier for you?'

Another movement of her right hand.

'Back in a tick.'

She was on her way back to the cubicle with a glass of water when a man came up to her. 'I believe you're looking after my wife? Lydia Rivers?' he asked, sounding anxious.

She nodded. 'I'm just bringing her some water. She's OK—she has a chest infection.'

He closed his eyes briefly. 'Oh, God. Not another one.'

There was definite pain in his voice. But he wasn't hurting for himself—he wasn't like Jonathan, irritated that his wife wasn't well and it wasn't convenient for him. This man knew what his wife was going through and hated the idea of the woman he loved being in pain.

'I'm writing her up for antibiotics,' Emma said, 'but I'm going to refer her to the neuro team. And maybe we can have a bit of a chat, with your wife's permission—you've recently moved here, yes?'

He nodded. 'New job. I wasn't going to take it, but she insisted that I shouldn't put my career on hold just because she's ill.' He swallowed hard. 'We know we're on borrowed time.'

She knew that feeling. Well. When every day seemed to

speed by and you just weren't ready to say goodbye. 'And you want to make the most of what you've got left.'

He swallowed hard. 'Yeah.'

Mrs Rivers's eyes welled up with tears when she saw her husband. He sat on the bed next to her and slid his arm round her, propping her up. 'All right, angel? That's comfortable for you?'

'Yeah. Doctor…knows,' she whispered. 'Under…stands.'

'Mrs Rivers, if I have your permission, can your husband answer questions for me about your health?'

Mrs Rivers moved her right hand.

'Thank you. Mr Rivers, I know your wife was diagnosed three years and eight months ago. Is it ALS?' Amyotrophic lateral sclerosis was the most common form, starting with weakness in the limbs, but all forms eventually led to breathing and swallowing difficulties.

'Yes. Lydia's finding it harder to get around, so we made sure we moved to a bungalow when we came here.'

'To keep as much independence as you can.' She'd done the same thing. She sat on the other side of the bed and took Mrs Rivers's free hand. 'It's frustrating, because your mind and your senses aren't affected at all. Just your body won't do what you want it to do because the nerve cells aren't working properly and can't send the messages from your brain to your muscles.'

'Hate it,' she whispered. 'Burden.'

'You're *not* a burden. Absolutely not.' Emma shook her head. 'Trust me on this one. Your family love you and they're trying to make the most of the time they have with you.' Just as she had with Lucy.

'It's true, angel,' Mr Rivers said.

'Now, obviously you haven't seen the neuro team here yet, but has your new GP got you on physio sessions?'

Mr Rivers shook his head. 'Not yet.'

'We'll get that sorted. Breathing exercises can help a lot.'

'We saw on the internet you can get a breathing machine,' Mr Rivers said.

Emma grimaced. 'It's not a cure. And although it helps, yes, you can get dependent on it—which will mean you'll be house-bound, Mrs Rivers, and it'll drive you crazy, feeling stuck in one place all the time. The neuro team here's very good and they might have some alternatives.'

'Drug trials?' Mr Rivers asked hopefully.

'There are a few going on, yes. But not just drugs. Just little things to make your life more comfortable and improve the quality of your life. Actually, aromatherapy's good.'

'Isn't that—well, a bit…flaky?' Mr Rivers asked.

'Keep an open mind,' Emma advised. 'There have been trials showing that lavender oil really helps people relax and removes some of the stress. These sorts of things are always worth a go. But the thing I'm really concerned about today is the swallow-ing.' She squeezed Mrs Rivers's hand. 'I'm sorry for asking your husband here rather than you, but it's not because I think you're not capable of answering. I know that when you've got a chest infection and your breathing's bad it's a big struggle to talk, so, please, don't think I'm ignoring you.' She looked at Mr Rivers. 'Has your wife lost a lot of weight lately?'

'Yes. I make sure whatever I cook is soft and should slip down easily, but she finds it hard to swallow.'

'And that means it's even harder to eat a balanced diet and get the right nutrition.' She nodded. 'When you see the neuro team, ask them about the options for a PEG.'

'What's that?'

'It stands for percutaneous endoscopic gastrostomy. Basically it's a tube that goes through a tiny hole in the wall of your abdomen. The neuro team can do it under local an-aesthetic—they use a flexible telescope that goes through your mouth into your stomach so they can get the PEG in the right place. It doesn't hurt, and it means you can have a liquid diet without all the hassle of swallowing.' She looked at Mrs Rivers. 'And because you'll be getting all the right nutrition, you'll feel a lot better, too. And if they can build you up a bit it'll help with your immune system and you might not be prone to quite so many chest infections.'

'Last time Lyd ended up in Casualty—when she had a fall— they didn't seem to know much about MND,' Mr Rivers said. 'Unlike you.'

For a moment, she almost told them about Lucy.

Almost.

It still hurt too much.

She forced herself to smile. 'I have friends on the neuro team.' Which was true. Just not the whole truth. 'Look, I can write you up some medication to deal with that chest infection, but I think you'd be much better cared for in the neuro department—they can write you up for the same things but, more importantly, they can talk to you about your treatment now and maybe see if there are things that can help you a bit more and give you a bit of independence.'

'That's the worst thing—Lyd not being able to do things for herself, even simple things. We don't mind helping, but *she* minds.'

'Because it's frustrating. You feel useless and your self-esteem takes knock after knock. And you don't believe anyone can possibly value you any more.'

'We value you, Lyd,' Mr Rivers said, tightening his arm around his wife.

She pulled the mask off. 'Love you. Strangers…my voice… hard. You…knew…hand.'

Emma nodded. 'Because that's a way of letting you communicate easily when it's hard to talk. And, yes, strangers would find it harder to understand you than your family because of the changes in your voice.'

'It's different with you because you're a doctor and you're used to it,' Mr Rivers said.

'Something like that.' She stood up. 'I'm going to call the neuro team now. Someone will come down to you, and they'll take you up to the ward. They shouldn't be too long, but there's a drinks machine in the reception area, Mr Rivers, if you need it. And if you need anything at all while you're waiting, just give one of us a yell. Don't worry about us being busy. That's what we're here for.'

He gently moved his arm from round his wife's shoulders, stood up and held a hand out to Emma to shake. 'Thank you,' he said. 'Thank you so much. You've made this a hell of a lot better for both of us.'

'That's what I'm here for,' Emma said, taking his hand and shaking it. 'Good luck. Though you don't need it because I know I'm leaving you in the best hands.'

And she blinked back the tears as she left the cubicle.

CHAPTER SIX

Rob, who'd been working in the next cubicle and had heard a lot of what Emma had said to her patient, didn't get a chance to talk to her until their next break. And then—knowing that if he gave her the chance she'd evade the subject entirely—he decided to ask her a direct question. 'I overheard you with the patient Kirsty called you to. How come you know so much about MND?'

She shrugged. 'Maybe I did a rotation in neurology in my house officer year.'

A suggestion, he noted, rather than an outright lie—but not one he was going to accept. 'That'd be highly unusual. Rotations are usually in the emergency department and then somewhere like Paediatrics or Obs and Gynae—and the stuff you were talking about wasn't just clinical, it was day-to-day living. And not just the sort of things you'd know from having friends working in the specialty either.' He folded his arms. 'There are two ways we can do this, Emma. The hospital grapevine here is good. Very good. I only need to go and ask one person a question—and you know *exactly* who I'll ask—and I'll get a whole slew of answers. Or…' He paused. 'Or you can tell me yourself.'

Her eyes widened. 'That's blackmail.'

'Nope. It's called letting someone in.'

'That's rich, coming from *you*,' she muttered.

He smiled. 'That's why I'm the best person for the job, honey. Because I understand exactly where you're coming from.' He didn't let anyone in either. Hadn't since Natasha. Because he knew that if you let people too close you got hurt— and the emotional scars were a hell of a lot slower healing than the physical ones.

Which was exactly why he shouldn't be getting involved here.

But how could he stand by and just watch the pain shimmering in those beautiful green eyes? 'Come on. I'll shout you a hot chocolate in a quiet corner of the canteen. And don't argue.'

'Chocolate?'

'With whipped cream. And cocoa sprinkled on the top,' he tempted.

'Do you know what that stuff does to your arteries?' she asked.

'Yup, but considering you have a dog whom I assume you take for regular walks or runs—not to mention your work on the mountain rescue team—I don't think your arteries have anything to worry about regarding a single mug of hot chocolate.'

She pulled a face. 'I loathe whipped cream. Especially the stuff they use here—it's from a can.'

'OK. I'll order it without.'

She shook her head and sat down. 'I'm not really in the mood for hot chocolate.'

The fact she'd sat down made him think that she was prepared to tell him. Ask a direct question and you got a direct answer. 'So why,' he asked softly, 'do you know so much about MND?'

She swallowed hard. 'Because my sister had it.'

'Lucy?'

She nodded. 'She was a graphic artist at a big advertising agency in Manchester. And then one day she noticed she was having problems gripping her pencil and doing fine detail work, so she went to her GP to check it out. She had a string of tests—and she was diagnosed with MND when I was in my last year of training.'

Rob noticed her use of the past tense. He knew that Emma lived on her own. And he also knew that the average life expectancy after diagnosis of MND was three to five years—some people lived a lot longer, others less.

So he was prepared for Emma's quiet addition. 'She died just over a year ago.'

'I'm sorry' was meaningless. He hadn't known Lucy. But right then he ached for Emma. 'Cases like Mrs Rivers—even though we don't see them in the emergency department much—must hurt. Bring it all back.'

'A bit,' she admitted.

He could tell she was only just managing to keep the tears back. And it made him want to hold her close, let her draw strength from him. 'Hey.' He pulled her to her feet and hugged her.

She pulled away. 'Don't, Rob. I'm OK.'

The slight quaver in her voice told him otherwise. 'No, you're not.'

'I'll be fine. I can manage.'

He sighed. 'Look, let's go out for dinner tonight. Somewhere quiet. We can talk properly.'

She shook her head. 'Can't. Byron's been on his own all day. And even though my neighbour feeds him for me when I'm on a late, it's not fair to leave him.'

'Let's get a take-away and go back to your place, then. **My** shout.'

'Thanks for the offer, but no.'

She clearly wasn't going to let him close. 'Whoever he was, he really did a number on you,' he said softly. 'Not all men are like that.'

'Not all women are like your ex,' she retorted, 'but that hasn't stopped you refusing to have another relationship that lasts longer than two dates.'

'True.' He kept his gaze fixed on hers. 'As I said earlier, maybe we could be good for each other.'

'And maybe,' she said, 'I like my life exactly as it is. Leave it, Rob.' She walked to the door. 'I'll catch you later.'

He didn't push it, knowing that she needed space. But he had no intention of leaving it there. Emma was hurting. And for the first time in years he wanted to be close enough to someone else to make them feel better. He wanted to make Emma feel better.

And it scared the hell out of him.

The following morning, despite sleeping badly, Emma was up early for her usual run with Byron. But even the run, followed by scrubbing her kitchen floor, didn't dispel the feeling of restlessness. The feeling of being coiled up so tightly that she was going to explode.

When she found herself pacing around the house, Byron nudged her knee.

'Yeah. I know. I need to do something. Something to take my mind off it.' She rummaged in the kitchen cupboards. 'And the scent of vanilla helps.' The scent that took her back to her childhood, to memories of making fairy cakes with her mother in the middle of the afternoon so they'd be cooling on the rack but still warm from the oven by the time her big sister came home from school. Days when they'd been so happy.

Today she couldn't face making fairy cakes. But a few batches of muffins would do. Using the out-of-season blueberries she'd bought on impulse from the farm shop the previous morning. Even though she was off duty today, she could maybe drop in at the hospital and leave them a few muffins.

Climbing.

That was what Rob had planned to do on his day off. He'd been looking forward to it all week. He'd even worked out exactly where he wanted to go, how long it'd take him and, since it was a solo climb, the time he'd brief his mother to call the local mountain rescue team for help if he hadn't phoned her by then.

Except he found himself driving in a completely different direction.

This was ridiculous.

Emma might not even be at home. It was her day off, too, and he had no idea what she did in her spare time. Maybe she'd be out on a long walk with her dog. Maybe she'd be meeting friends for lunch. Maybe she'd be out shopping. And even if she was home, maybe she'd slam the door in his face.

Stupid, stupid, stupid.

He was setting himself up for rejection.

He shouldn't even be considering this, let alone doing it.

But he couldn't help himself. The impulse was way too strong to resist. So he stopped off at the florist and bought the nicest bunch of flowers he could find. Drove to the village where Emma lived and parked outside her home. And when he saw a window open in the front, he knew she was definitely there. It was unlikely she'd have left a ground-floor window open while she was out.

She might turn him away.

Then again, she might not.

And, anyway, he'd never been a coward.

He locked his car, then rang the front doorbell.

Emma frowned as she heard the doorbell ring. Nobody ever rang her front doorbell. Everyone always came round to the back of the house and knocked on the kitchen window—if she was in, the back door was always open.

Odd.

She wasn't expecting any deliveries or anything.

But she turned the hob down so the pan wouldn't boil over and went to the front door. And blinked in surprise when she saw Rob: he was the last person she'd expected to see.

'Hi.' He smiled at her. 'I was just passing.'

Considering she lived on one of the back streets in the village, they both knew that wasn't strictly true. She folded her arms. 'Really?'

'I was thinking about going climbing.'

'Uh-huh. The car park for the nearest climbing hotspot is about five miles away,' she pointed out.

'I know. I'm taking the scenic route.' He whipped one hand from behind his back. 'All right. I admit it—I wanted to see you. And I thought you might like these.'

He handed her a gorgeous bouquet of white flowers: roses and freesias and gypsophilia.

'They're lovely.' When was the last time anyone had bought her flowers—especially ones that looked and smelt as wonderful as this? She couldn't remember. 'Thank you.' Belatedly, she remembered her manners and took a step back. 'Come in. I'll put the kettle on.'

'Something smells nice.' His eyes widened when he saw the muffins cooling on a rack. 'You made these yourself?'

'Making muffins isn't exactly rocket science.'

'Making good ones is. And these ones smell delicious.'

She smiled and filled a vase with water. 'They're blueberry. Help yourself,' she said as she began arranging the flowers.

He didn't wait to be asked twice. 'Mmm. These taste as good as they smell,' he said after the first bite. 'You're definitely a woman of many talents.'

'Oh, stop flannelling me.' But a warm glow was spreading inside her.

'Tell her she's a good cook,' he advised the dog. And then

he looked up at her. 'Um, is he allowed a little tiny bit?' He waved the muffin at her.

She sighed. 'He shouldn't, but OK. A little tiny bit won't hurt. Be warned, he's very greedy.'

Byron took the morsel daintily, as if to make her out a liar, and Rob laughed. 'You *fraud*, Byron.' He glanced back up at Emma. 'My parents' Labradors are just the same.'

'You grew up with dogs?'

'Yes. And I really missed having a dog around when I lived in London.'

He'd worked in London for four years—and his climbing accident had been five years ago, so he must've moved to London after he'd got his mobility back again. Presumably to get away from memories of his ex-fiancée. 'Where did you work before London?' she asked.

'Leeds. So I used to go into the Yorkshire Dales whenever I could. Walking, climbing.'

'Until your accident.'

'Hey. I'm fine now. Though I have some amazing scars.' He gave her a wicked grin. 'I'll show you, if you like.'

'Are you ever serious?'

'About some things.' His smile faded. 'But one thing I learned in that hospital bed: life's very short, and you only get one chance at it. And I want to grow old and know that I laughed at least once every single day.'

'That's a nice philosophy,' she said, handing him a mug and sitting down at the scrubbed pine table.

'And you thought I was just another shallow party animal.' He pulled out the chair next to hers and sat down.

'That's how you come across.'

'And you come across as way too serious.' He placed his mug on the table, leaned over and lifted the corners of her mouth with his thumb and forefinger. He narrowed his eyes, then shook his head and removed his hand. 'No, I think I prefer the natural way.'

She couldn't help smiling—it was such a ridiculous thing for him to have done.

'Re-*sult*! Gimme a high five, Byron.' He bent down, lifted the dog's paw and whooped.

She rolled her eyes. 'Oh, for goodness' sake. It's not that big an issue.'

He shrugged. 'Sometimes when people get hurt, they react by going quiet and keeping everyone at a distance—and they need someone to remind them they're still part of the human race.'

'And others go off the rails—they burn the candle at both ends and keep their lives so full, they don't have time to sit and think about how they're feeling,' she retorted.

'Don't forget I had months when I couldn't do anything else except lie in bed and think about it,' he reminded her. 'And all that pent-up energy had to go somewhere.'

'So a month of being in plaster equals, what, a year of partying?'

'Sounds about right to me. Though I could do a month in plaster equals a decade of partying. Yeah, that'd be even better.' He glanced up and saw the cork board on one wall full of pictures. 'Is that Lucy?'

'Yes.'

He left the table and walked over to take a closer look. 'She's very like you. This is a nice one.' He indicated a photograph of Lucy holding Byron as a puppy. 'She obviously liked dogs.'

'Yeah.'

He clearly sensed that she was holding something back because for once he was quiet, waiting for her to talk. When she didn't fill the silence, he wandered over to the stove and peered into the pan whose contents were bubbling away. 'Bright purple? Interesting.'

'It's beetroot and cumin soup.'

'Funny, I didn't have you pegged as a cook.'

She shrugged. 'I enjoy it. It's relaxing.'

'Smells good. Earthy and spicy at the same time. I don't think I've ever actually tried beetroot and cumin soup,' he remarked.

Knowing it was a bad idea—knowing that she really ought to make an excuse and put some distance between them—she asked, 'Why don't you stay for lunch and try it?'

He stared at her. 'You're inviting me to lunch?'

Clearly he thought it was mad, too. OK. She'd tell him she'd changed her mind.

Except her mouth wasn't working from the rulebook. 'Yes.'

His smile was slow and sweet and did seriously disturbing things to her insides. 'Thank you. I'd really like that.' He leaned against the worktop. 'Home-made soup and home-made muffins. Hmm. Any chance of home-made bread to go with it?'

'Not made by me, no.'

'Oh.' He looked disappointed.

'Anyone ever told you that you're pushy?'

'Me?' he said with a grin. 'No.'

And then he resumed pacing her kitchen. He was hardly ever still, she noticed. Restless. Prowling, almost. Still a reaction to being cooped up in plaster all those years ago? Not that there was any point in asking. She knew he'd deny it.

'Is there a bakery in the village?' he asked.

'There's the farm shop.'

'Where is it?'

'The other end of the village—the big barn on the left just as you're on your way out to the Dales. Why?'

He rolled his eyes. 'You're a smart cookie. Work it out.' He stood in the doorway to the hall, then intoned, 'I'll be back,' in his best impersonation of Arnold Schwarzenegger.

And then he gave her an impertinent wink.

How could she resist laughing? 'Don't bother ringing the doorbell when you come back,' she told him. 'Come round the back. The kitchen door's unlocked.'

'Yes, ma'am.' He sketched a salute and left.

When he returned, ten minutes later, she'd blended the soup.

'You wanted bread, you said.' She looked at the packages he unloaded onto the table. Ham carved off the bone, two types of local cheese, local butter and a pot of organic relish.

'Ah, well. You didn't tell me the farm shop had a deli as well as selling home-made bread. And I've just joined their box scheme—they start delivering to me next week, but in the meantime I have lovely dirty vegetables sitting in the back of my car. Food with *flavour* that hasn't been washed in chlorine and wrapped in plastic. Yum.'

'My fridge isn't empty, you know. You really didn't need to buy anything for lunch.'

'Well, I wanted to make a contribution.' He smiled. 'C'mon. You've provided the soup, the muffins and the coffee. So I'm merely providing the bit in between. Breadboard? Knife?'

He wasn't giving her a second to think. She gave in and took the breadboard from the cupboard and the knife from the drawer. By the time she'd poured the velvety soup into two bowls and brought them to the table, he'd cut bread and laid everything else out on plates. Made himself completely at home in her kitchen, she thought, as if he'd always been there.

Which was a seriously dangerous thought.

She didn't need anyone in her life. She was perfectly happy as she was.

'Perfect feast,' he said. 'And this looks fantastic. You definitely need a white bowl to appreciate the colour of that soup.' And then he tried it. 'Wow. This is seriously good. Even better than it looks.'

'Thank you.'

'Though I imagine,' he said, 'you have a huge repertoire of soups and smooth sauces.'

'Mmm.' She bit into a hunk of bread to avoid answering.

He clearly guessed her strategy, because he waited until her mouth was empty before saying, 'You know, I never pictured you living in a modern bungalow.'

She frowned. 'What do you mean?'

'I thought you'd live in a really old stone cottage.'

She'd thought about it. Before she'd qualified. But it hadn't worked out that way. 'I wanted somewhere without stairs.'

'So Lucy could keep her independence?' he guessed. 'It was good of you to look after her.'

She frowned. 'Of course it wasn't. I didn't do it to be *good*. She was my sister and I loved her. I wasn't going to dump her into a care home. Besides, she did the same for me.'

Rob said nothing. He just waited. Right now he had a feeling he'd just pushed Emma over a boundary—and she'd be out of sorts enough to tell him what he needed to know.

Finally she took a deep breath. 'Lucy was ten years older than me. Our parents were both doctors, and when I was fourteen there was this big earthquake out in Mexico. They'd both worked for Doctors Without Borders before Lucy was born, and they'd stayed in touch with their old colleagues. Some of them were going out to help and Mum and Dad wanted to do their bit, too.'

Was that why Emma had become a medic? he wondered. Because of her parents? But he didn't interrupt. Didn't want to give her the excuse to stop talking.

'It was the summer holidays, so Lucy offered to take a week off and I went to stay with her up in Manchester while Mum and Dad went out to Mexico.' She stared down at the soup. 'It was meant to be for just a week. Except in the middle of the rescue operations there was another earthquake. Nearly all the rescue workers were killed.'

'Including both your parents?' Rob asked softly.

She swallowed hard. 'Yeah. They were both only children, so that left just me and Lucy. She offered to find a job in Sheffield and move back down to live with me so I wouldn't have to move schools, but she'd only just been promoted at work so I didn't think it was fair—besides, I wasn't starting my GCSE courses until September. It wasn't as if I was in the middle of a crucial year or anything.'

'So you moved up to Manchester?'

She nodded. 'Though her boyfriend wasn't too happy about it.' She swallowed. 'I wasn't even a rebel or a wild child who made his life hell. Just an ordinary schoolgirl, one who probably spent too much time with her nose in a book. But I guess he didn't like having to share Lucy's attention with me.'

Rob could guess what was coming next.

'He made her choose between him and me. And she said anyone who'd ask her to do that wasn't worth choosing.' She bit her lip. 'They'd bought a house together, so Lucy bought him out with her share of the money from selling our parents' house.'

'And you went on to do your A levels and med school,' he said. 'Did you do your medical degree in Sheffield, by any chance?'

She nodded. 'It's got a good reputation as a teaching hospital. I enjoyed it there.'

'And Lucy was diagnosed with MND in your last year.'

'My year as a house officer.' She nodded. 'I offered to finish my training in Manchester so I could help her out a bit. She wouldn't hear of it because she knew I loved it here—besides, by then she was married.'

And yet Emma had been the one to look after Lucy in the final stages of her illness. Rob had a nasty feeling he knew why Emma was so wary of men. Lucy's husband had obviously bailed out, too—and now Emma clearly thought that men were unreliable. He couldn't ask her straight out, not if it'd rub salt in the wounds. So he asked softly, 'Her husband looked after her?'

'You must be kidding.' Emma made a noise of disgust. 'I always thought Jonathan was a bit full of himself but that he was basically harmless. And I believed he was looking after my sister—until I took a day off and just popped up to see her, as a surprise.' Her face tightened. 'I found Lucy in tears. And that's when she admitted to me that things weren't good between them. Hadn't been ever since her diagnosis. Jonathan was pleased that she'd had to give up the mountain rescue work—he liked the idea of his wife doing charity work, but the fact she could be called out at any time annoyed him. But it wasn't just the rescue team that she lost. She couldn't do her job any more either. And he really, really resented that. Resented losing half their income, because the disability benefit was nowhere near what she'd been earning. So they couldn't afford to just fly over to New York for the weekend any more. Skiing was out, too. And she got too tired to party. Found it hard to walk in high-heeled designer shoes.' She gritted her teeth. 'It turned out he was having an affair—he claimed he felt trapped, and Lucy wasn't well enough to meet all his masculine needs.'

Rob could barely believe what he was hearing. No wonder Emma found it hard to trust. Even Natasha hadn't been that cruel. 'That's the worst excuse I've ever heard,' he said.

'Oh, it gets better.' Her voice was bitter. 'He'd always told Lucy he wanted to wait to have kids—and she went along with him, even though she wanted a baby and she'd have been a brilliant mother—and then suddenly his girlfriend was pregnant. And of course he had to stand by her because she needed him… As if Lucy didn't.'

'What a bastard,' Rob said, feeling his fists tighten.

She grimaced. 'I lost it. I'm afraid I drove up to his office and confronted him. In front of everyone. And I said that my sister deserved far, far better than a coward who'd sleep around and then walk out on her when she needed him most. That's when he said he couldn't face a lifetime of being tied to a cripple.'

Rob flinched. Words he'd heard before. And he'd been on the receiving end. 'Just like Natasha, when we weren't sure if my spine was going to be OK.'

'Yeah. I think those two would deserve each other,' Emma said feelingly. 'Anyway, I smashed his laptop at that point.' She bit her lip. 'I pretended it was his face.'

'Pity it wasn't.'

'He wasn't worth it.' She toyed with her soup. 'He was furious. Said he'd sue me. Except everyone in his office said they hadn't seen me do a thing and he had no witnesses—it would be his word against mine and they'd give me an excellent character in court.'

'Good for them.'

Emma swallowed. 'They all knew Lucy, as an ex-colleague and a friend. And then one of them told him what I couldn't bring myself to say—that Lucy wouldn't actually be around for a lifetime. Just for a few years. So that "cripple" remark…' She shook herself. 'It makes me so angry, even now. Anyway, no way was I going to leave her to his supposed "care". I packed all her stuff that afternoon and took her back to my place. Rented the first bungalow I could find.' She spread her hands. 'Better still, after we'd settled in, I persuaded the owners to sell it to me, so there weren't any problems modifying the place. I could have the odd rail or two put in and changed the path so it was a ramp instead of a step.'

'And you've got good neighbours?' he asked.

'The best. Joan and Rita kept half an eye on Lucy for me while I was at work—not enough to make her feel useless, but

I didn't have to worry so much. And the neuro team at the hospital are brilliant. We managed just fine without Jonathan and Damien.'

Now there was a name he hadn't heard before. 'Damien?'

'My ex.' She shrugged. 'Lucy wasn't very good at picking men. Neither am I. Damien claimed I was sacrificing my life for Lucy just because of some stupid idea that I owed her for looking after me when I was a kid.'

Rob frowned. 'Hardly. Of course you'll be there for someone you love when they need you. So he asked you to choose between them?'

'No.' But he'd asked questions. Asked if she could have MND, too. Asked if any children they might have could develop the disease.

She'd been honest with him.

And he hadn't liked the answers. He'd looked at her as if she were some kind of freak. As if it was all her fault.

Even now, the memory made her throat feel tight. 'He asked me for his ring back.'

'You were engaged to him?' At her nod, Rob reached over and curled his fingers around hers. 'Please, tell me you told him to get lost and flushed his ring down the toilet.'

She gave him an unwilling smile. 'No. I was so disillusioned by that point, I just took it off and handed it to him.'

'Ouch. I take it he wasn't a medic, then, seeing as he didn't understand Lucy's condition?'

'Merchant banker.' She gave him a wry smile. 'And a complete idiot.'

He laughed. 'You know, you're full of surprises. The woman who doesn't climb for fun is a key member of the local mountain rescue team. And now I find the woman I thought was quiet and sweet and demure is one tough cookie with the ability to smash up someone's laptop.'

She lifted a shoulder. 'Well…'

'So the mountain rescue stuff—you're doing that for Lucy, aren't you?'

'I suppose so.' She bit her lip. 'Lucy always wanted to do SARDA work. But Jonathan didn't like dogs, so she stuck to the normal Pennine rescue team. And obviously she couldn't work on the Fellside team when she moved here—her mobility wasn't good enough. But she did a bit of comms work when she was having a good day, and she helped me train Byron. Strictly speaking, I should've been on the team for a long while before I even started the SARDA training. But Lucy's old team leader put in a word for me, said that Lucy had been brilliant and I'd follow in my big sister's footsteps.'

'And you have,' Rob said softly.

'I hope so.'

'Do you feel better for telling me?'

'Yes. No. I don't know.' She blew out a breath. 'What I really want to do right now is take the dog for a walk. Talking about Jonathan always makes me angry—and I need to get rid of the frustration.'

'Want some company? My walking boots are in the car.'

She looked at him. 'Yes and no.'

'Yes, if I shut up and don't probe?'

She nodded. 'And I think you should stop holding my hand.'

He left his fingers exactly where they were. Still curled around hers. 'You seem to have a bit of an identity problem, where I'm concerned,' he said softly. 'Confusing me with men in your life who've behaved less than honourably. I think you've worked out I'm not another Jeremy. So I'd like you to know that I'm not another Damien either.'

'You look like him. Tall, dark and handsome.'

'You think I'm handsome?'

She felt her eyes narrowing. 'Stop fishing. You know you're good-looking.'

'I'm not going to answer that. If I say yes, you'll say I'm arrogant, and if I say no you'll say I'm being falsely modest. That,' he said, 'is slightly worse than asking me if your bum looks big in those jeans.'

'Does it?'

He grinned. 'I'm not answering that one either. And I hope you can't read minds. Otherwise you might slap me.'

She wriggled her fingers out of his grasp. 'Just go and get your boots.'

CHAPTER SEVEN

BY THE time Rob had changed into his walking boots, Emma had already locked the house and Byron was trotting along beside her on his lead.

'What about the washing-up?' he asked.

She made a dismissive gesture. 'There isn't much. I'll do it later.'

If he made a fuss about it, she might change her mind about the walk. And he really wanted to spend some time with her. So he simply smiled and joined her on the walk.

It was a glorious day, very mild with a really blue sky. The air was clean and sharp. When they rounded the top of the hill and Rob saw the valley sloping down below them, he just stopped and stared. 'This is amazing. No wonder you moved here.'

She shrugged. 'Serendipity. It was the right house and the right place. I was just lucky.'

'I don't think I'd ever get tired of this view,' he said.

There was something else he didn't think he'd ever get tired of either. Though he wasn't quite ready to admit it to himself, let alone to Emma.

They walked in companionable silence for a while.

'Do you miss Leeds and the Dales?' she asked.

'Not now. And I still go back—my parents live in Pickering, at the bottom of the North York moors,' he said.

'So the rocks where you fell… Have you climbed in the area again?'

'Twice,' he told her. 'The first time my palms were sweating all the way and my heart was going at twice its normal rate. I could still remember the feeling of the handhold giving way, of my foot slipping and then crashing down because I hadn't roped myself properly. But I had to do it. Prove to myself that I wouldn't let it beat me, that I could still climb. And when I got to the top, it was the most incredible feeling. I'd beaten the fear. So I abseiled down and did it all over again.'

She stared at him. 'I'm not sure if you're brave or mad.'

He laughed. 'I think the jury's still out on that one. So why don't you like climbing?'

She shrugged. 'It's not my thing.'

'Did you fall?'

'No.'

'You saw a bad fall, then?' he probed.

She rolled her eyes. 'I'm a volunteer on the rescue team. Of course I've seen bad falls. Or, at least, the results of them.'

'What, then?'

'It's just not my thing.'

Her tone was light, but Rob heard the warning: she wanted him to back off. Part of him itched to slide his arm around her shoulders, hold her close and tell her it didn't matter. But he knew it wouldn't be enough for him—he wanted to kiss her again, as he had the night of the rescue.

And if he did, he knew she'd run a mile.

This was definitely something he needed to take slowly. She'd already told him she always picked the wrong man: and he wanted her to know he most definitely wasn't the wrong man. That she could trust him not to behave the way Damien had—or her sister's husband, for that matter.

But their conversation had settled something for him. Since

Natasha, he'd always steered clear of a permanent relationship. Hadn't wanted to risk it with someone who couldn't commit.

Caring for someone with MND proved Emma had commitment. That she wouldn't shy away if things got tough.

So maybe with Emma it would be different. Maybe with Emma, the risk of a relationship wouldn't be like climbing a sheer gully without any ropes. Maybe with Emma, this whole thing would work.

He switched the conversation to something innocuous, and gradually she relaxed enough with him to start chatting, pointing out areas of interest in the distance.

'I've never really explored the Peak District. I did most of my climbing in Yorkshire,' he said. 'And I suppose because I had a good climbing area on my doorstep, I didn't bother coming to explore here.'

'You'll probably find it different here. The White Peak area's limestone and the Dark Peak is gritstone,' she explained. 'Though they've both got their share of steep climbs, I think the White Peak has the edge because of the limestone caverns—the formations of stalagmites and stalactites are incredible.'

'So you prefer caving to climbing?' he asked, intrigued.

She shook her head. 'I'm with the tourists there: I'll take the guided tours only. I don't fancy crawling around in muddy passages where it narrows to the point where I'm not sure I can get through, or suddenly coming across a huge lake and the only way out of the cave is underwater—when I have no idea how deep it is or how long I'm going to have to swim before I can come up the other side.' She shivered. 'Luckily the Fellside team callouts are all outside rather than in the caverns and potholes.' She looked at him. 'Why do I get the nasty feeling you'd just *love* that sort of thing?'

'You said it yourself. I'm either brave or mad.'

'Why do you do it?'

He smiled at her. 'Because it makes me feel alive. Seeing how far nature can take me. Meeting the challenges.'

'Mad. *Definitely* mad,' she said.

But she was smiling. So maybe there was hope.

When they got back to her house, it was dusk, and Rob was surprised to realise they'd been out for more than three hours. 'Sorry. I've hogged almost all your Saturday—in half an hour it'll be too dark to do anything.'

'I didn't have that much planned. Just tackling the ironing Everest.'

He grimaced. 'Now, that's one mountain I *really* don't like tackling.'

'And yet you walk onto the ward with a perfectly crease-free shirt every time.'

She'd noticed such a little thing about him? Funny how that made him feel warm inside. 'I'll let you into a secret. I have a laundry service just to iron my shirts for work. It's the first thing I sorted out when I moved into my flat.'

'That's so *decadent*.'

He spread his hands. 'No, it's necessary. It takes the stress off my bad leg.'

She coughed. 'Considering you're on your feet all day in the department—not to mention climbing, and the fact you've just been out on a three-hour walk with me—I don't think that excuse washes. And wasn't it *two* bad legs, not one?'

He laughed. 'All right. I admit I could iron my shirts myself—but then again I can pay someone to do it, then spend the time I would've spent ironing doing something much more fun. If you look at it like that, it's an easy decision.'

'As I said, you're a party animal.'

Maybe. But he had a serious side, too. One he hoped she'd see for herself. 'Well, thanks for the walk. I enjoyed it.'

'Yeah. So did the dog.'

She didn't say anything about whether she'd liked being out with him, too. Or maybe he was trying to run before he could walk. Hoping the disappointment didn't show in his face, he dropped to his haunches and made a fuss of Byron. 'See you later, beautiful.' He looked up at Emma. 'Thanks for your hospitality. I'll see you at work on Monday, then.'

'Yes. Hang on a minute,' she added.

Hope flared. Was she going to ask him in again?

But then she disappeared indoors while he changed out of his walking boots, and returned with a carrier bag. 'The remainder of the stuff you brought for lunch,' she said, handing it to him.

'No need.'

'My fridge is well stocked and I'd hate to deprive you.' Was it his imagination, or was there the tiniest sparkle in her eye? 'There's something else in there, too.'

Rob glanced inside the bag. 'Muffins? Oh, you're a wonderful woman. I could kiss you for that.'

And he almost did. Except he saw the flicker of worry in her face.

'I *could*,' he added, 'except for the fact that we have a no-kissing friendship.'

The relief in her expression really shouldn't sting that much. Was he such a lousy kisser? He hadn't had complaints from any of his previous girlfriends.

Then again, he hadn't met a woman like Emma before.

And she wasn't actually his girlfriend.

'Enjoy the rest of the weekend,' she said.

'Cheers—you, too.'

Emma stood on the doorstep and watched Rob drive away. Weird how her house suddenly felt all big and echoey and empty without him.

This was ridiculous.

She'd been living on her own for a year now, just her and the dog, and it was fine. Today had been the first time Rob had been inside her house. They were just colleagues—after all, she'd known him for less than a week. No way should he have this kind of importance in her life so soon.

'You need your head examined,' she told herself loudly.

She glanced at Byron, whose sad spaniel face looked just that little bit sadder. Droopy.

So she wasn't the only one.

'Yeah. I feel that way a bit,' she said softly, and sat on the floor so she could make a fuss of him. 'I know you liked him but I can't do this, sweetheart. I can't get involved with Rob.' She sighed. 'I have this rubbish track record with the male of the species, present company excepted—and I don't want to be that vulnerable again. Ever.'

Byron pressed his nose into her hand and shifted closer to her.

'I'm already on dangerous ground. I've virtually bared my life to him—I can't take any more risks. I can't let him closer.' She rested her cheek against the spaniel's soft fur, and Rob's words echoed in her head.

I'm not another Damien.

Maybe she was being unfair, not giving him a chance. Maybe he'd be the exception to prove the rule and he wouldn't let her down.

But it wasn't just the fact she had trust issues. She had to bear in mind that Lucy had died from motor neurone disease.

Around five to ten per cent of cases of MND involved a genetic component. And Emma didn't know whether Lucy had been one of that group. Hadn't had any tests herself to see if she carried that same genetic marker. The chances were she wouldn't develop it—but there was a fairly high chance she was a carrier. Which would mean not having children, in case she passed it on to them.

That had been the final straw for Damien. The reason why he'd left.

So even if she did allow herself to trust Rob, could she really ask him to do the thing Damien had refused to do—sacrifice having a child of his own? And if the answer was no and he walked away…

No, it was better to keep things as they were. Colleagues, acquaintances. Not too close.

Emma gritted her teeth and tackled her ironing pile, deliberately putting something upbeat on the stereo to improve her mood. Though it still didn't shift her feeling of being at a loose end. Neither did a sybaritic bath with the expensive honey-scented bubble bath she favoured, lit by candles and with chill-out music wafting through from the living room. And although she curled up on the sofa with Byron to watch a film later that evening, her heart wasn't in it.

Sunday was just as bad. Particularly when she dropped in to see her neighbours, bearing muffins.

'That young man who called in to see you yesterday seemed nice,' Joan commented.

'He's a colleague—one of the other doctors in the emergency department,' Emma said.

'What's his name?' Rita asked.

'Robert.'

'Ooh. Like Robert Redford,' Joan said. 'Except with dark hair, of course. But just as handsome. Didn't I say he was dishy, Rita?'

'You did. And they were very nice flowers he brought you, Emma,' Rita said. 'Roses are expensive at this time of year, you know.'

Emma hid a smile. Her elderly neighbours missed absolutely nothing. But she wasn't going to take umbrage or accuse them of interfering, because they'd been good to her since the day she and Lucy had moved in. They'd kept a distant but still vigilant eye on Lucy, so they had been within hailing distance in case she'd needed them but without making her feel helpless when she was managing well. And even now they kept Emma's spare key so they could let Byron out and feed him when she was on a late shift. 'Yes, they're very nice,' she said. 'But, really, Rob's just my colleague. He's recently moved to the area and I'm about the only person he knows right now. That's why he popped in to see me.'

'Hmm,' Joan said, sounding completely unconvinced. 'Men don't usually bring flowers to their *colleagues*.'

'They do if they have impeccable manners,' Emma said sweetly.

'You've been on your own a while now, love. It's time you found yourself someone special and settled down,' Rita said.

Which was absolutely not going to happen, Emma thought, but didn't have the heart to tell them.

'Lovely girl like you—you need a family,' Joan added.

'Hey, I've got Byron and you two. And the Fellside rescue team. And that does me just fine,' Emma said. And then she played her trump card, the one that always worked when that particular subject came up and she needed to escape before she said something to hurt their feelings. 'I'll go and put the kettle on, shall I?'

Emma was half-dreading work on Monday. But Rob treated her just like he treated everyone else in the department. He was completely professional, making sure the whole team worked together. At the same time he managed to charm all the patients with his attention to detail, and all the nurses and junior staff because he treated them with respect instead of the disparagement they'd always had from Jeremy.

Over the next couple of days, Emma began to relax. This was

going to work. She could work with Rob just as friends, suppress these little flashes of desire. Everything was going to be fine.

And then it was the mountain rescue team's training evening, the following Wednesday, when Rob had agreed to finish off his talk and then join them all afterwards in the pub.

'Don't you go sliding off home, young lady,' Ken said, putting his hand on her shoulder at the end of the training session. 'You know they allow dogs in the Crown. And Byron's never any trouble. Do you want a pint, lad?'

Byron woofed.

'See? He said he'd have "arf",' Ken claimed, grinning.

'That's a terrible joke. And you are *not* turning my dog into a beer monster,' Emma warned, laughing.

'Didn't say beer, love. I said a *pint*.' Ken winked at her. 'And in his case it's "arf" a pint of Adam's ale. Water.'

Somehow she ended up sitting next to Rob, squashed against him on one of the wooden pew-like benches. Thigh to thigh. She could feel his bodily warmth through two layers of denim.

'One girly beer, as requested,' Ken pronounced in disgust, setting the bottle down before her. 'You really don't know what you're missing, Em.'

She eyed the dark, thick-looking liquid in his glass with distaste. 'Oh, I think I do.'

Rob, to her surprise, had also opted for half a pint of real ale. Along with the rest of the men who'd joined them from the team. Tonight she was the only female present. Only a handful of them had gone to the Crown, because the others had all had prior claims on their time.

'While we're here and I've got most of the ones I need,' Ken said, 'I want to talk about our annual fundraiser. We do a panto in the primary school's hall every Christmas, Rob,' he explained for the newcomer's benefit. 'Three performances, and they're always packed. This year we're doing *Cinderella*. And the wife's given me a cast list.' He took the large briefcase from under the table and took out a thick wad of scripts. 'She's the fairy godmother, of course.'

'Well, of course,' Dave said. 'Considering she normally waves the magic wand known as the radio.' Alison, Ken's wife, was their communications specialist.

'Dave, you're an Ugly Sister.' Ken handed Dave the script. 'And so are you, Geoff.'

'Who's Buttons?' Rob asked.

'Me,' Ken said with a grin. 'We've got Henry as Baron Hardup, Pete as Dandini—and it's obvious who Cinders is.' He smiled at Emma and pushed a script across to her.

'Oh, puh-lease.' Emma rolled her eyes and started glancing through the script—then burst out laughing. 'Alison's written a real cracker here. So who's Prince Charming, then?'

'Gotta be the new boy, hasn't it?' Ken said, and handed Rob a script.

He had to be kidding. They wanted *Rob* to play Prince Charming?

Maybe he'd turn the part down. Say he was too busy at work.

'Better let me know when the performance dates are so I can make sure I'm off duty,' Rob said.

Oh, no.

She knew the story. It meant she'd have to dance with Rob on stage. Up close and personal. And kiss him at the end.

OK, so it would be a stage kiss. And with just about anyone else on the team, that would've been absolutely fine.

But Rob had kissed her properly. Intimately. Until her blood had felt like champagne, fizzing through her veins.

How on earth was she going to kiss him on stage and stay sane?

'I assume you can sing?' she asked Rob.

'Doesn't matter if he can't—we'll just get Alec to sing and Rob can mime,' Ken cut in.

If she didn't know better, she'd think that the Fellside rescue team had joined her neighbours in a campaign to get her a man to settle down with. In the shape of one Robert Howarth.

'I can sing. Not pop-star standard, but not out of key.' Rob shot Emma a sidelong look. 'I used to be in the choir at school.'

'You were a choirboy?' Dave guffawed. 'Yeah, right. You have that angelic look about you, Rob. Not.'

Rob laughed back. 'Trust me. Is there a score with this, then, Ken?'

Ken looked surprised. 'Sure. I'll get the wife to run one off for you.' He blinked. 'Blimey. We've actually got someone in the panto who can read music, apart from Alison?'

'There's no end to my talents,' Rob said, breathing on his nails and polishing them on his fleece.

'Says the man who pays people to iron his shirts,' Emma cut in.

'Because he hasn't got a wife to do it for him. Actually, seeing that Cinderella's supposed to do all the housework and what have you, and you're—' Ken began.

'No. Absolutely *not*. It's bad enough doing my own,' Emma said, laughing. 'And even if I were married—and I have no intention of making that mistake—I'd make my husband do his own ironing, thank you very much.'

For a second her gaze met Rob's. And there was a distinct challenge in his blue, blue eyes.

Oh, help.

'Well, that's settled. Bridget's going to do the costumes and play the piano for us—Bridget's the headmistress of the primary school, Alison's boss,' Ken explained for Rob's benefit. 'The kids are going to do our backdrop, and basically we just have to learn our lines and turn up for rehearsals.'

Rob was laughing as he read through the script. 'I can't

believe how many mountain rescue jokes you've managed to get in this. And since when does Cinderella have a dog?'

Byron, as if recognising his cue, woofed under the table, making them all laugh.

When Emma had finished her drink, she wriggled out of the pew. 'Right. That's me done for tonight—I have some lines to start learning.'

'Are you walking home?' Rob asked.

She made a dismissive gesture. 'I normally do.'

'As it's raining, I'll give you a lift. Save you getting soaked.'

She was aware that everyone in the team was watching them with interest. If she made a fuss and refused, they'd notice—and they'd ask questions. So it was much easier to smile politely and accept his offer.

'See you later,' Rob said, scooping up his own script and following Emma out of the pub.

Byron leapt into the back of the car as if he did it every day and was completely used to it. And when Rob parked outside Emma's house, he said quietly, 'Are you OK about me being in the panto?'

'Why wouldn't I be?'

'Because I don't want you feeling that I've muscled in on your territory.'

'No, it's fine.'

'Good.'

Even though the only light outside was from the headlamps of Rob's car and she couldn't see his face properly, she knew he was looking at her mouth. Remembering the last time he'd kissed her. Thinking of the fact he was going to have to kiss her on stage.

Her mouth went dry. 'Thanks for the lift,' she muttered. 'I'd better let you get on. See you at work.'

Politeness meant she ought to invite him in. But she couldn't. Dared not. Not while she was still thinking about kissing him.

'Goodnight, Em,' he said, and, as usual, waited until she'd opened the front door and was safely inside before he drove off.

There was a definite conspiracy here, she thought. Rita had been the lollipop lady at school for years—and she and Joan always did the door collections and the tickets on the night of the panto. And, given that the village had an even more efficient grapevine than the hospital, Alison and Ken and the rest of the Fellside team probably knew that Rob had brought her flowers the previous weekend.

They probably even knew which route she and Rob had taken on their walk.

And if they'd decided that Rob ought to be her real-life Prince Charming, it had only been one step away from casting him in the panto. Which they'd done.

She sighed. They all meant well, she knew. But it wasn't going to happen. Rob had as many emotional scars as she did. It would never work.

And she'd have to find a way of letting them all down gently.

CHAPTER EIGHT

THINGS were definitely weird, Emma decided. Rob had been working at Fellside General for over a month now, and he hadn't gone on a single date. Rumour had it that he'd turned down Mel in the radiology department when she'd suggested going out for a drink. And Stacey, the surgical registrar who'd taken a shine to him when she'd come down to discuss a case and asked him out for dinner.

It wasn't that Rob had given up partying. He always seemed to be the first one to suggest a team night out, and he'd arranged a ten-pin bowling night and a curry evening. He'd been the first one to sign his name on the list for the team Christmas dinner. And she knew he was socialising in the Crown with the Fellside team, too, because whenever one of them saw her they casually mentioned him and then started singing his praises.

But as for his reputation for dating women twice and then ending the relationship…he hadn't dated anyone at the hospital.

Not even once.

So was the grapevine wrong, for the first time ever? Or was something else going on?

'Penny for them?' Rob asked, walking into the staffroom.

'What?'

'Your thoughts.'

'Oh.' She felt the colour flood into her face. No way was she going to tell him she'd been thinking about him. Wondering why he wasn't dating anyone. 'They're probably not worth that much.'

He made himself a coffee. 'Had a good morning?'

'Yes. You?'

'Reasonable.' He smiled. 'You know, I still can't believe we have a pantomime dog instead of a pantomime horse.'

'Not to mention climbing boots instead of a glass slipper.'

'So does the panto usually raise a lot of money?'

She nodded. 'And I hope it happens this year, too. We're aiming to raise enough for the other half of a new Land Rover ambulance.'

'Do you just sell tickets in the village?'

'No, we sell them here as well. Ruth normally has a sign up in Reception and keeps a stock of tickets and the float money in her filing cabinet. A lot of the staff here go, because they know the Fellside rescue team.'

'So we'll have a friendly audience, then? Good.' He paused. 'We've got a rehearsal at the school hall tomorrow night. As I don't actually know where the school is, shall I pick you up so you can direct me?'

'It's smack in the centre of the village. You can't miss it.'

'It'll save carbon emissions, too, if we take one car instead of two. Not to mention car parking spaces.'

'I was going to walk,' she said.

'Ah, but as Cinderella you'll need practice at getting in the glass carriage—getting in my car will be just as good. And if it's raining…'

She smiled. 'I'm used to rain. I don't mind getting wet. And we're not having a glass carriage.'

'If I don't give you a lift, everyone will think we've had a fight. And you don't want Joan and Rita asking you what I've done to upset you, do you?'

'That,' she said, 'is blackmail.' Somehow he'd managed to meet her neighbours. And they hadn't stopped talking about him since, or hinting that he was such a nice young man and just the sort she needed. To the point where it was driving her bananas.

'So I'll pick you up at a quarter to seven?' he asked.

She really didn't have much choice, so she gave in gracefully. 'A quarter to seven it is. Thank you.'

At half past six, Rob parked outside Emma's house. He walked round to the back and tapped on the kitchen window before opening the kitchen door and calling, 'Hello?'

'Be with you in a minute,' she called back. 'It's not time to go already, is it?'

'No, I'm slightly early.' Because he'd wanted to spend just that little bit more time with her. Any excuse. How pathetic was that? he berated himself.

'Feel free to make yourself a coffee, if you want one.'

'Thanks, but I'm fine.' He made a fuss of Byron, then looked at her photo board again. Pictures of her parents—she and Lucy both looked like their mother—pictures of her and Lucy, pictures of herself with the rescue team and what looked like the day she and Byron had qualified for SARDA work. Lucy was there, too, smiling despite obvious pain, leaning on a stick.

In that particular photo, Emma's smile was a mile wide. She looked proud and happy and full of life. The Emma he'd met seemed a much quieter version. She still smiled, but there wasn't that extra sparkle.

Loneliness, maybe?

He knew how that felt. Days of lying in a hospital bed, knowing that the future he'd planned had crumbled into dust. The wedding was off, and because he'd been physically unable to do much a lot of the burden of cancelling things had fallen on his mother. And while he'd lain there, getting used to the fact that life would never be the same again, he'd sworn he'd never, ever let himself feel lonely again. That he wouldn't get close enough to anyone to let them hurt him like that again.

So why, he wondered, was he so drawn to Emma? Why, when he knew her emotional scars were as deep as his and she'd find it just as hard to trust, was he trying to spend as much time as he could with her?

Probably, he thought wryly, because Emma Russell was like no other woman he'd ever met. Beautiful, clever, caring—and with integrity, in spades. Given the way she'd looked after her sister, he knew that Emma was a woman he could rely on. A woman who'd never, ever let him down. And that, together with the way that just catching her eye could make tingles run down his spine, made her irresistible.

Except he was clearly far from irresistible to her.

And if he pushed her too far, too fast, he'd blow this.

He needed to take things carefully. Hold himself back. Be patient.

She emerged from the bathroom, her hair still slightly damp.

Rob's fingers itched to slide into the soft silkiness, the way they had the night he'd kissed her. But he held himself back and schooled his face into a friendly smile. He wanted her to feel easy in his company, not wary.

'Ready to go?' he asked.

'Sure.'

As usual, Byron jumped into the back of the car and lay quietly until he'd parked again. And the rehearsal was fine until the moment when Prince Charming had to dance with Cinderella at the ball, and kiss her just as the clock started to chime midnight.

It was meant to be a stage kiss. Something that looked like a proper kiss, but wasn't. And yet the second her mouth brushed against his, he forgot what he was supposed to be doing. Forgot that this wasn't for real. Kissed her properly.

And she kissed him back.

Time stopped.

Rob felt as if he were walking on moonbeams. No, as if he were *dancing* on moonbeams. With Emma in his arms, kissing him like this, anything was possible.

And then he was faintly aware of whistling.

Whistling that became louder. Wolf whistles. Cheers. Cat calls.

Oh, hell.

He was kissing Emma. In a completely inappropriate environment. In front of half the Fellside search and rescue team.

Alison coughed. 'She's meant to leave when the clock strikes midnight! I make it...' she tapped her watch '...somewhere about half past three.'

He hadn't been kissing her that long.

Not for hours and hours.

Had he?

Rob's face felt on fire. And Emma was blushing, too. Right to the roots of her hair.

'And this is supposed to be a family performance,' Ken added, grinning.

Rob spread his hands. 'Hey, Prince Charming is meant to kiss Cinderella. What did you expect?'

'Tell you what we didn't expect,' Alec called. 'To need a fan!'

Rob laughed. 'I suppose space blankets are more the order of the day for the rescue team. Except in summer when inexperienced walkers go out without enough water and get heatstroke. So let me get this timing right—Prince Charming stops kissing Cinderella *before* the last stroke of midnight, yes?'

'So she can drop her glass slipper,' Alison said with a smile.

'Got it.'

During the scene where the Ugly Sisters tried on all kinds of boots before finally admitting that the glass slipper—otherwise known as Emma's climbing boot—was five sizes too small, everyone was laughing so much that the kiss was forgotten.

Rob hoped.

They had a post-rehearsal drink in the Crown—Rob stuck to half a pint of beer, mindful that he was driving—and finally he drove Emma home.

'Um…would you like to come in for a coffee or something?' she asked.

Or something—now, there was a thought.

But he knew she'd only asked him in out of politeness. He wanted more than that. A lot more. 'Thanks, but I'm fine. I could do with an earlyish night, actually—I've got a bit of a drive tomorrow.'

'Tomorrow?'

'I'm heading up to Pickering to see my parents on my days off. It's three-quarters of an hour or so, the other side of York,' he told her. He smiled. 'Better than the London journey used to be. In the end I used to go by train because it was quicker. At least here it's drivable.'

'Have a safe journey,' she said.

'Thanks. I'll, um, see you back at the hospital, then.'

'Yeah. See you.'

Emma was really, really glad she and Rob were both off duty for the next two days. They really needed some space between them. And she needed some time to straighten her head out—especially after that kiss.

According to the script, it was just a stage kiss. Prince Charming and Cinderella. But when Rob had kissed her, she'd completely forgotten where she was. Forgotten about the audience, until the wolf whistles and cat calls had seeped into her consciousness.

What worried her most was that she was beginning to fall for Rob. He was completely Mr Wrong. Even though he wasn't living up to his 'two dates and that's it' reputation, she knew he wasn't looking for commitment. And she didn't want to be let down again. Better to keep her life as it was.

Their next shift together was a late shift, and Rob didn't see Emma until the middle of the afternoon. Though he was well aware of every time she walked past whichever cubicle he was in, treating a patient. Even the sound of her voice made his nerve-ends tingle with longing.

He really had it bad.

He'd spent two days just missing her. To the point where his mother had taken him gently to one side and asked him straight out about the woman who was on his mind.

A woman who'd been let down as badly as he had.

But one he trusted. As a doctor, as a member of the rescue team…and as something more?

He'd suggested a fling to get it out of their systems. Emma had said no. And she was dead right, he thought—a fling wouldn't be enough.

So maybe he needed to take a risk.

But she didn't trust him. Didn't trust any man, except on a professional level. What would make her trust him enough to give him a chance?

'Hi. How was Yorkshire?' she asked, when she met him in the corridor.

'Fine, thanks.'

He really wanted to kiss her. Brush his mouth against hers. Breathe in her sweet scent. Hold her close.

But he forced himself to sound calm, friendly, as if she were just another of the team. 'How were your days off?'

'Fine, thanks.'

'Any callouts while I was gone?'

'One. A man who was known to be depressed—the police had found his car abandoned three days before, but there was no sign of him. It was a pretty big search—they had teams from the two nearest MRT centres as well as us.' She pulled a face. 'Bit grim, because we thought we might be searching for a body.'

He made a sympathetic noise. 'What happened?'

'Ken's lot found a sheep skull and two footballs. I was with Geoff and Dave, and we didn't find anything at all. When we got back to Control, apparently the police were picking up a signal from the man's mobile in the next valley, so we were stood down. And they found him later on that night.'

'Good. Glad it was a successful end.'

'Me, too. Especially getting this close to Christmas. I mean, there's never a good time to lose anyone, but Christmas always seems harder.'

Christmas. It was only a couple of weeks away now. Although apparently they didn't tend to decorate the emergency department, apart from a small Christmas tree behind the desk in Reception, everyone was thinking about the holiday season. Planning parties, time off to spend with family. Not to mention the 'bran tub', where you picked someone's name out of an envelope and bought them a secret gift which was handed out by the consultant on Christmas Eve.

He'd hoped to pick Emma's name, but his luck was out. And if he'd tried to fix it, the hospital grapevine would've started chattering and she'd be embarrassed. Even more than when he'd kissed her so thoroughly at the panto rehearsal.

'Yeah. It's tough on people.' He was just about to ask her what she was doing for Christmas when he heard his name being called.

Barbara was at the other end of the corridor, looking worried. 'We've got a child with a high temperature who's just gone into fits in Reception. Can you…?'

'On my way. Catch you later, Emma.'

Their last case that evening was a man who'd drunk too much, got into a fight and ended up falling through a window. The paramedics had brought a sample of the glass in.

'Excellent,' Rob said. 'We're going to X-ray the wounds and the glass at the same time.'

'Why?' Emma asked.

'Little trick I learned in London. Glass shows up in different ways on X-ray—if it's over a millimetre thick, it should show up and we can be confident that we've got most of it out. But if the sample glass is invisible on the X-ray, we need to be extra careful when we examine and wash out the wound, to make sure the glass is all gone.'

Following the X-ray, Emma sketched out a diagram for the sites of the wounds—mainly on the arms—and noted the measurements Rob called out. 'Incised wounds,' she wrote on the notes, 'contaminated by dirt and glass.' Which meant possible tendon injury.

'OK, mate. I need to do a couple of checks before I can give you some pain relief,' Rob said.

Though, judging by the amount of alcohol fumes from the man's breath, anaesthesia was hardly going to be necessary.

''Sall right, Doc. You do what you have to,' the man slurred.

The shock of falling through the window had probably been enough to take the fight out of him, Rob thought with relief.

'Em, you move the joints while I check the wounds,' Rob said. 'Not that I don't think you can do it, but partial tendon division is easily missed.' When they'd finished, he nodded. 'Tendons fine. Distal pulses?'

She checked them. 'Fine.'

'Good. There's no sign of sensory loss.' The guy must have been so relaxed by his alcohol consumption when he'd gone through the glass that he'd been lucky. Incredibly lucky.

'OK, mate. I'm going to put some local anaesthetic in, get the glass out, then clean your wounds and stitch them.'

'Fine, Doc.'

'And I'm going to give you a tetanus shot, just to be on the safe side.' Even though the wounds weren't heavily contaminated with dirt, were less than six hours old and the tissues weren't devitalised, some of the incisions were deep—meaning they'd be more prone to tetanus. 'Can you remember when you last had a tetanus shot?'

'Couple o' years back.'

Rob wasn't entirely convinced, but he'd make a note to contact the man's GP.

Then the man gave them a beaming smile and started singing Christmas pop songs, completely out of key and with half the words changed to 'la la la'. Clearly he was usually a 'happy' drunk rather than an aggressive one—and had been caught up in the fight rather than starting it.

Rob caught Emma's eye. She, too, could see the funny side of this. Out of a sense of mischief, he winked at her.

To his surprise, she winked back.

He fished out the glass then washed out the wounds and started suturing them.

'Blimey, if Alison could see how fast and neat your stitches are,' Emma told him, 'she'd have you working on the costumes.'

'Yeah, yeah.' But the compliment pleased him.

When he'd finished stitching, he put a dry, non-adhesive dressing over the wounds. 'This should keep them clean for the next couple of days,' he told the patient. 'You need to rest and elevate your arms for the first twenty-four hours. But if you get any redness, pain, swelling or fever—or you see any sign of red streaks on your arms—you need to come back here straight away because it means your wounds are infected and we need to treat you.'

'Sure, Doc.' Rob was rewarded with a beaming smile.

'Make an appointment to see your doctor in about ten days so he can take the stitches out,' Rob advised.

'And we've got a leaflet here about wound care—take it home and have a look at it tomorrow,' Emma suggested.

Rob gave her a grateful look. For cases where alcohol or drugs were involved, the patient often couldn't remember what had happened the next day—let alone any detailed instructions about wound care. Instruction leaflets were invaluable.

After the patient had left, he finished writing up his notes. When he walked into the staffroom, Emma had already taken her things from her locker and was clearly on her way home.

'Em, before you go…'

She paused. 'Yes?'

'Have dinner with me tomorrow night?'

'Thanks for the offer, but no.' Her eyes were very clear. 'I'm not in the market for a relationship.'

Too far, too fast. He backtracked quickly. 'What about friendship? Look, I'm still the new boy around here.'

She gave him a disbelieving look. 'You must be joking. You're always out socialising.'

'Which isn't the same as having a good friend.' He sucked in a breath. 'I like you, Emma.' More than liked her, but he'd keep that to himself for the moment. 'And you made me lunch.'

She made a dismissive gesture. 'Hardly—I'd already made the muffins and the soup.'

'But you still cooked me lunch. So I'd like to cook you dinner. Tomorrow night, as we're both on an early shift.'

'What about Byron?' she asked.

He spread his hands. 'If you have dinner with me at seven, you'll have time to feed him and give him a walk between the end of your shift and me picking you up.'

She frowned. 'Why are you picking me up?'

'Because it's easier than giving you directions to my place.' And she was less likely to beg off at the last minute.

She was silent for so long that he couldn't bear it. 'Please?' he asked softly.

'I...' She bit her lip.

'It's dinner, Em. Just dinner. And if you want to bring the dog as a chaperon...well, I'm not supposed to have pets, so if my landlord decides to call round, we'll just have to hide him.'

To his relief, the ridiculous suggestion made her smile. 'OK. Dinner. And I won't bring Byron, in case it upsets your landlord.'

'Great. See you tomorrow.'

Tomorrow, he thought, suddenly held all sorts of possibilities.

CHAPTER NINE

DINNER.

What did you wear for dinner?

It had been so long since she last dated, she couldn't remember. Then again, this wasn't officially a date.

'Help. I don't know what to do,' she informed Byron. 'He said "as friends". So do I wear something casual, as I would if I were going to supper at Kirsty's?'

The spaniel lay with his nose on his paws, just looking at her.

'If dogs could speak, you'd definitely be saying "dunno",' she said wryly, crouching down to stroke the top of his head. 'He's making an effort tonight, cooking for me. So if I go in jeans and a sweater, that's saying I'm not bothering to make the same effort. Which is rude.'

Byron licked her hand.

'But wearing a little black dress would be way over the top.' Or would it?

In the end, she compromised. Wore the black shift dress she hadn't worn in heaven knew how long. Dug out a pair of high heels from the bottom of her wardrobe—shoes she'd ignored for so long that they were dusty and needed a good clean before she could wear them. But she left her hair pulled back, the way she wore it at work, and used only the lightest sheen of rose-pink lipstick and a single coat of mascara.

So it didn't really count as dressing up for a date—did it?

When she opened the door to Rob, she had to swallow hard. He looked gorgeous.

Wearing a round-necked black top and black trousers—not jeans, she noted—he looked good enough to eat. His hair was still faintly damp from the shower and he'd clearly shaved—she only just stopped herself reaching out and finding out for herself how soft his skin was.

'Hello, beautiful.'

Her stomach swooped with pleasure—until she realised he was talking to the dog.

Well, that was what she'd wanted, wasn't it? She'd said she wasn't in the market for a relationship. So she shouldn't be disappointed that he'd taken her at her word. What was the saying? *Be careful what you wish for: you might get it.*

'Hi, Emma. Ready?' he asked.

She nodded, checked the dog's water dish was full and settled him on his bed, then picked up the bottle of wine she'd bought earlier and locked the door behind her.

Rob, like her, lived reasonably near the hospital, though the block of flats where he lived was on the edge of urban sprawl rather than being in one of the little Peak District villages. His flat was on the third floor of the four-storey building.

'Welcome,' he said quietly when he'd unlocked the door, standing aside so she could go in first.

He'd left a light on in the little entrance hall so she could see to take her shoes off. The entrance hall had several doors leading off it: to a small galley kitchen; a living room; a bathroom and—presumably behind the closed door—his bedroom.

'It's rented,' he said, 'so it's not quite my choice in décor, but I'll start house-hunting after Christmas. There's no point in looking seriously now, with the holidays coming up.'

'Wrong time of the year,' she agreed. 'So have you sold your place in London?'

He shook his head. 'I rented it out—furnished—so virtually nothing in here belongs to me.'

'It's a nice flat,' she said. It gave absolutely no clues to Rob, but the décor was unobtrusive and inoffensive—cream walls, beige carpet and curtains, beige sofa and pale wood furniture. The pictures on the walls were the sorts of landscapes you'd find in just about any hotel—nothing anyone would object to, but nothing that said *this is my home* or *this is who I am*. Bland on top of bland.

She handed the bottle of wine to him. 'My contribution to dinner.'

'Thank you.' He smiled at her. 'May I offer you some wine?'

'Thanks, that'd be lovely.' And having a glass to fiddle with would do a lot to settle the butterflies in her stomach.

'Red or white?'

'White, please.'

He poured her a glass from a bottle of sauvignon blanc that was already chilling in the fridge, but he didn't join her, pouring himself a glass of sparkling mineral water instead.

'I'm driving you home afterwards, so I'm only having one glass of wine—and I'm saving it for dinner,' he said with a smile, as if he'd noticed the surprise on her face. 'And I promised I wouldn't keep you out late. Come and sit down.'

The dining table in the living room was set beautifully, she noticed, with a proper tablecloth and napkins. He'd obviously gone to some trouble.

As she sat on the sofa, she noticed there were no books around to give her a clue to his tastes—no films either, though he had a state-of-the-art TV and a seriously good sound system. Then again, there weren't any shelves in the flat to house books or films or music. Most of his stuff was probably either in storage or still back in London.

'No CDs?' she asked.

He shook his head. 'My music's all on a hard disk.' He picked up a remote control and pressed a couple of buttons—and music flooded the room. A soft, jazz-type piano with female bluesy vocalist: real chill-out stuff.

'This is lovely,' she said.

'Good. Enjoy. I'm just going to fiddle with a couple of things in the kitchen,' he said. 'Back in a minute.'

Should she go and offer help? He'd more or less hinted that she should stay put, but she felt awkward just sitting here on the sofa, turning the stem of the wineglass round and round in her fingers.

Emma stood up and walked over to the mantelpiece and looked at the framed photographs. There was a picture of Rob and an older couple who were obviously his parents, and another with a man who looked so like him that he must be Rob's brother and a woman who had the same beautiful Celtic colouring but her features were a more feminine version of Rob's: clearly his sister.

It was obvious from the love in their faces and the warmth of the hugs that Rob was close to his family and they adored him.

A lump filled her throat. How much she missed her own parents, her sister. Being part of a family. Being loved for who she was, regardless.

But, as things were, she wasn't going to be part of a family. Wasn't going to settle down and have kids—not with the shadow of MND hanging over her.

She blinked back the sudden sting of tears. This wasn't a pity party. It was dinner. As friends. And it was time she stopped mooching about.

She walked through to the kitchen. 'I know you said to sit down, but I'm a natural fidget. It doesn't feel right to be just sitting there.' Besides, when he'd had lunch at her place, he'd been as involved as she'd been in the preparations. 'Can I do anything to help?' Or was he a territorial cook, preferring not to share his kitchen?

'Thanks for the offer, but it's all done. It's just a matter of waiting for the potatoes to boil so I can turn the heat down.'

There was a pan of new potatoes on the hob, and green veg sat in an electric steamer on the worktop. 'Something smells nice,' she said.

'Chicken in white wine and mushrooms.' Then he looked at her in horror. 'Sorry, I should've thought to check first. When we had lunch, you ate cheese rather than ham. You're not a vegetarian, are you?'

She smiled. 'No.'

'And you're OK with fish?'

She laughed. 'Anyone would think I had a reputation for being picky! Yes, I like fish. Though I admit mussels aren't my favourites.' But if he served mussels, she'd eat them. She wasn't going to be a princess about it.

He looked relieved. 'I haven't done mussels. Well, don't be polite. If I serve up anything you hate, just leave it. I won't be offended.' He turned the potatoes down as the pan started bubbling. 'Right, this lot should do by itself for a while. I'll come and join you.' He shepherded her back to the living room. And then he really surprised her: he struck a match and lit a dozen or so candles, then turned out the overhead light. The candlelight was soft, yet there were enough candles to make the room reasonably bright.

'We'll start eating in about ten minutes,' Rob promised.

By the time he brought the starter through—and insisted on seating her at the table, in an old-fashioned gesture that surprised her—she'd relaxed.

'This is fabulous,' she said after her first mouthful of the creamy smoked salmon mousse.

His smile made the corners of his eyes crinkle. 'I'd better

tell you now, I bought it from the deli. But I did cook the rest of the food.'

'Rob, we're friends.' Even as she said it, she realised it was true. She couldn't put her finger on exactly when it had happened, but they'd somehow become friends. She enjoyed working with him at the hospital and on the rescue team. Looked forward to seeing him. 'You really didn't have to go to this much trouble—a supermarket pizza and a bag of ready-prepared salad would've been fine.'

'You must be joking. That's the kind of thing I eat on my own,' he said. 'There never seems much point in cooking just for one. But cooking for more than one…that's worth it. Actually, you've done me a favour—my daily consumption of fruit and veg-etables will be a lot better today because I'm cooking.'

She wasn't sure if he was teasing or not. But the main course was fabulous. And the pudding…

She stared. 'A white chocolate fountain?'

'Yup.' He produced a bowl of strawberries and another of raspberries to go with the chocolate. 'They're out of season and, yes, I feel a bit guilty because I know I should be buying things seasonally and locally, where possible, but I love strawberries and raspberries. And together with white chocolate…' He scooped one from the bowl and dipped it in the chocolate fountain. 'Bliss. It doesn't get any better than this.'

'Completely decadent,' she teased, but followed suit.

Her fingers brushed against his as she dipped the straw-berry into the chocolate, and the light touch sent a shiver down her spine. She couldn't help meeting his gaze. And when he bit into the strawberry she found herself wondering what his mouth would feel like against her skin.

This was crazy.

She'd come here just as friends.

The idea of being lovers should be far from her mind.

And she definitely shouldn't be noticing that tiny smear of chocolate on his lower lip. Or thinking about leaning over to lick it off.

It was even worse when they'd had their fill of the fruit and he brought in two cups and a cafetière of rich, strong coffee—along with the most gorgeous chocolates she'd ever tasted.

'My secret pleasure,' Rob said with a grin. 'I would do almost *anything* for these.'

Lord, his mouth was sexy. And his comment had put the most incredible pictures in her mind. Of feeding him chocolates, bite by bite, between kisses. And—

She gulped her coffee, willing the caffeine to wake up her common sense.

It didn't work.

The combination of candlelight, chocolate and one of the most beautiful men she'd ever seen was way too much for her common sense.

She made one last try at it. 'Can I do the washing-up for you, seeing as you cooked?'

He shook his head. 'There isn't that much.' He paused. 'But you can do something for me.'

'What?'

'Dance with me.'

His voice was a husky whisper. The ultimate temptation. And even though she knew that friends didn't dance together to the kind of music he was playing, songs with a slow and sensual beat—the kind of music that lovers danced to—she couldn't say no. She tried. Opened her mouth, about to suggest that maybe she should go home and check on her dog. But the word 'yes' came out instead.

With manners more impeccable than those of a maître d', he pulled her chair back and drew her to her feet at the same time. Then he spun her into her arms and held her close.

Her arms slid round his neck; one of his hands was flat against her spine and the other was resting on the curve of her buttock. She could feel the warmth of his body; she was close enough to feel his hard musculature against the softness of her curves and to breathe in his clean personal scent.

This was crazy. They really shouldn't be doing this. There was no future in it.

But she couldn't help swaying with him in time to the music, closing her eyes and leaning against him. She wasn't really listening to the tracks. All her senses were filled with Rob, the feel of his body so close to hers, the sound of his breathing, the scent of his skin.

And she was lost.

He'd dreamed about this.

Virtually since the moment he'd first met Emma.

Holding her this close.

In his arms.

All woman.

All *his*.

The dress she was wearing was beautiful, but all he wanted to do was take it off her. And although he knew he ought to hold back, he couldn't help himself. He dipped his head so his mouth brushed the curve between her neck and shoulder. He loved her scent, the softness of her skin.

When she didn't pull away, he let his mouth drift over her skin up to her earlobe. 'You're beautiful,' he whispered. 'And I need to…' He slid one hand up to the place where she'd secured her hair and took out the scrunchie, let her hair fall loose and tangled his fingers in it.

Just as he had the night he'd kissed her in the moonlight.

'Your hair's so soft. Like silk. I know it's a cliché,' he said softly, 'but it doesn't mean it's not true. And I love the feel of it against my skin.'

She could remember the last time he'd done that. In the moonlight.

And then he'd kissed her.

On instinct, she turned her head so that her mouth brushed against his—the tiniest, lightest touch. And then they were kissing properly, hot and wet and hungry. Just as time had stopped when he'd kissed her at the pantomime rehearsal, it stopped again tonight—and this time there was nobody to cat-call and break the mood. Nobody to comment. Nobody else in the universe except the two of them.

Somehow her hands had burrowed under his top and were caressing bare skin. Soft, flawless skin over strong, hard muscles. Irresistible.

He dragged his mouth from hers for just long enough to ask, 'Emma, do you have any idea what it does to me when you touch me like this?'

It was hard to breathe, let alone speak. 'Pretty much the same as it does to me,' she said, her voice husky. She could feel his arousal, the hardness of his erection pressing against her—and her body responded in like manner, her breasts swelling to make her dress too tight.

'I want to touch you,' he said, his voice shaking, 'but I promised you tonight was just as friends, and I don't want you to think I make promises with no intention of keeping them.'

She shook her head. 'You're no schemer, Rob. But you once said to me,' she added softly, 'that it was going to happen again between us, and you didn't think we'll be able to stop it.' She dragged in a breath. 'And I think you're right. It is. And we can't.'

'I can't stop thinking about you, Em.' He nibbled her lower lip until she opened her mouth, then the tip of his tongue slid into her mouth, tasting her.

Desire rippled down her spine. She wanted him. Right here, right now.

'I can't stop thinking about you either,' she admitted when he broke the kiss.

'Neither of us does relationships,' he reminded her softly.

'I don't do flings,' Emma said. She took a deep breath. 'Neither have you. Not since you've been working at Fellside.'

Rob blinked. 'You noticed?'

She nodded. She'd noticed all right. And wondered. What if…? 'And the grapevine's buzzing about the dates you've turned down.'

He stroked her face. 'Want to know why?' When she didn't answer immediately, he said, 'It's because of you. You know Prince Charming doesn't want anyone except the one who fits the glass slipper?' At her nod, he said softly, 'I know exactly where he's coming from.'

From where she was standing right now, she fitted perfectly.

He brushed his mouth against hers. 'I want you.'

His pupils were so huge his eyes looked almost black. Deep and dark with desire. And the expression on his face made her blood heat.

She kissed him back. 'I want you.'

'Here?' he asked, sounding tortured. 'Now?'

'Yes,' she whispered, and his arms tightened round her.

'I want to do the caveman thing and carry you to bed.' He nuzzled her earlobe. 'But I want this to be mutual. So if you want to change your mind—for the sake of my sanity, do it now.'

'I'm not changing my mind.'

'Good.'

The feel of his breath against her skin made her shiver with longing. And when he lifted her hand and kissed each fingertip in turn, keeping his gaze firmly on hers, she could barely breathe.

'But there is something I need to do first.'

Her mind refused to function. She couldn't even begin to guess what it was.

Then he led her over to the candles at the far side of the dining table. Blew them out one by one, so the light slowly dimmed. Until he reached the last one, a pillar candle in a wrought-iron holder.

'The first time I kissed you,' he said softly, 'it was by moonlight. The first time we make love…'

Oh, such promise in his voice: *the first time*. Meaning that there would be other times?

'I want it to be by candlelight. I want to see you, Em. I want to watch the way your expression changes, see what pleases you and what takes your breath away.' He picked up the candle. 'And I can't wait any longer.'

CHAPTER TEN

EMMA had no idea how they got to Rob's bedroom. She couldn't remember walking and she knew he hadn't carried her. But then he set the candle on the table next to his bed—a king-size bed, she noted, with a wrought-iron frame. And she stopped thinking as he unzipped her dress and slid it from her shoulders.

She knew she was shaking. And his hands were trembling, too, as he stroked every inch of skin he uncovered.

'You do something to me, Em,' he said. 'Something I can't explain or describe, but it rocks my world.'

Yeah. She knew exactly how that felt. She finished untucking his sweater from his trousers, and tugged the hem upwards. He lifted his arms, letting her pull the garment over his head.

'Wow. Beautiful,' she said, her fingertips skating over the breadth of his shoulders and then across his chest.

'Me?'

'Uh-huh.' Washboard-flat stomach, broad shoulders, perfect musculature—and all from hard work and walking outdoors, not pumping iron in a gym.

'Funny, that.' He nuzzled her shoulder, and unclipped her bra with one hand. 'That's what I was thinking about you.' He let the garment fall to the floor and cupped her breasts in his hands, rubbing the pad of his thumbs against the hardened peaks of her nipples. 'Glorious.' He dipped his head and as she felt the slow stroke of his tongue against her skin, she dragged in a breath and slid her hands into his hair.

'I want to touch you,' he murmured against her skin. 'Taste you. Lose myself inside you.'

'I want that, too,' she said shakily.

He lifted his head for just long enough for her to see the twinkle in his blue, blue eyes. And then he gave her the sexiest smile she'd ever seen. 'Good.'

'You're wearing too much,' she pointed out.

He straightened up. 'I'm in your hands, honey. Do what you will.'

She undid the button of his trousers. Slid the zip down. Let the fabric fall over his hips. And then sucked in a breath as she saw the scars on his legs.

Rob froze. He knew the marks weren't pretty, but he'd grown so used to them that they didn't bother him any more.

But would they bother Emma?

Would they repel her?

Then he felt her fingertips trace them, very lightly. 'Rob. Do they…still hurt?'

'Not after this length of time. Though I get the odd ache here and there,' he admitted.

'That accident was really bad, wasn't it?'

'But it was years ago.'

When he took her hand and pulled her up, he didn't see revulsion in her face. Or pity. More a not-quite-sure expression, as if she didn't know what to say or do.

'And I healed a long time ago.' Physically, at least. And he'd overcome the fear, that first climb afterwards. Emotionally— he still wasn't sure that was going to happen. Emma was the first person in years who'd made him want to trust, want to try.

'Though I don't mind if you want to kiss me better,' he said, tracing the line of her jaw with the pad of his thumb.

'Is that a hint?' she asked.

He saw the teasing glint in those beautiful green eyes, and he smiled. 'Might be. Try it and see.'

The glint intensified, and she kissed the tip of his nose.

Oh-h-h. He hadn't thought it possible to want her even more. But he did. 'Wrong place.' The words sounded rusty, raspy— and it was a real effort to speak. To hold back and not just rip the rest of her clothes off.

'How about here?' She kissed his cheek.

'No.'

'Here?' She kissed the other cheek.

It was too much for him. He wrapped one hand round her waist, slid the other one across the nape of her neck, and kissed her thoroughly.

And then he deliberately fell back onto the bed, letting her fall on top of him.

'Better,' he said. Though she was still wearing too much for his needs. Gently, he hooked his fingers into the waistband of her knickers and her sheer black tights, and removed them both in one lithe movement, at the same time rolling her over onto her back. Got rid of the rest of his clothes at the same time. He didn't want a single strand of fabric between them: he wanted her close. Personal. Here. Now.

'Better still,' he whispered. 'You look amazing, with your hair spread out like that. And I want you more than I've wanted anyone in my entire life.'

She shivered. 'I… It's mutual.'

He had a good idea how much that admission must have cost her. He kissed her gently on the lips, then worked his way downwards. Traced a necklace of kisses around her throat. Moved down to nuzzle her breasts, drawing one nipple and then he other into his mouth until she was trembling. Stroked the soft undersides of her breasts, nuzzled her abdomen, gloried in touching every feminine curve.

And she gave him back everything he demanded: he could see exactly where and how she liked being touched, kissed. Stroked and touched and kissed her all over, stoking her desire, wanting her to feel as much as he did.

He only just stopped himself punching the air in triumph when the tip of his tongue pressed against the pulse point in her throat: her heart was pounding just as crazily as his own. She needed him as much as he needed her.

When he slid one hand between her thighs, cupping her sex with his fingers, she shivered.

'Yes.'

'Sure?'

She dragged in a breath. 'It feels as if every bit of my body is fizzing. As if I'm going to implode if you don't…'

Yeah. He knew exactly how that felt.

With shaking hands he took a condom from his wallet. It took him three goes to open the packet, but finally he managed it. Knelt between her thighs. And sank into her warm, sweet depths.

'You feel amazing,' he breathed.

'It feels pretty good from this side, too,' she said shakily.

'Only "pretty good"? Must try harder,' he said. And then his smile faded. 'Em. I want you so much, I don't think my self-control is going to be good.'

'Snap.'

She'd meant it was the same for her. But she may as well have been describing what had just happened to his self-control. He thrust harder, deeper, taking her up with him to the peak, until stars seemed to explode in his head and he cried out her name. He heard her answering cry, then felt her body ripple round his, little aftershocks of pleasure.

Emma had no idea how long they lay there, curled up together, cradled in each other's arms. But she didn't want to move, didn't want to speak and break such a perfect moment.

Rob was the one who finally spoke. 'You know I had this theory that a mad affair would get this out of our systems?'

'Yes.' She lay very still. What was he going to say? Adrenalin prickled at the base of her spine.

'I was so far in the wrong direction, I went off the map. And this isn't going to be enough for me. Not once, not twice,' he warned softly.

Be careful what you wish for. You might get it.

Right now she didn't know what she wanted. What she'd just shared with Rob had been breathtaking. More beautiful than anything she could've imagined. But did she want him in her life permanently? Did she want to risk giving him her heart, only to be let down—the way both she and Lucy had been let down by the men they'd loved?

Ending things between them now would hurt. Hurt like hell. But maybe it would be better to get it over with than to get even more deeply involved with him and end up being even more hurt in the long term.

But how did she tell him?

'I don't want us to go back to how we were. Colleagues. Friends. I want you in my life, Em.' He dragged in a breath. 'I don't know where this is going to take us. I'm rubbish at relationships. But with you, I want to try.'

She wriggled out of his arms—how cold the air felt without his body heat to warm her—and sat up. She drew her knees up to her chin and wrapped her arms around her legs. How could she let him down gently?

She took a deep breath. 'Rob, We got carried away tonight.'

'Just a tad.'

He was clearly trying for humour. To defuse the tension that was suddenly boiling round them like a stormcloud. But it wasn't working. Didn't make the fear go away. 'I don't know if I can do this.'

He sat up and put his arm round her shoulders, holding her close to him. 'Em, I know you've been hurt before. So have I. And I think we—'

He was cut off by the shrilling of a mobile phone.

'Yours,' he said. 'Do you want to get that?'

She shook her head. 'Whoever it is, they'll call back if it's urgent. Or leave me a message on voicemail.' She didn't want to drag this out any longer than she had to.

But then his mobile phone rang, too.

'The chances of us both getting a call at the same time… I've got a feeling about this. A bad one.' He dropped his arm from her shoulder and grabbed his phone from his bedside table. 'Hello?'

She waited. Who was it?

'Hi, Ken. Yeah. Am I available? Um…' He nudged Emma, who nodded without meeting his gaze. 'Sure. I'm on my way. Where's the RV? Uh-huh. Yes, it's OK, I've got satnav. I'll find it. I'll call you if I have a problem.'

As soon as he'd ended the call, Emma bit her lip. 'That call I missed—that was probably Ken.'

'Probably.' He looked grim. 'We'll finish this conversation later—and we *do* need to talk, Em. But for now we're both needed elsewhere. And, much as I want to say no to the rescue team and keep you here until we've sorted things out between us, we have responsibilities to other people—responsibilities we can't ignore.' A slight flush bloomed over his cheeks. 'I'll give you space to, um, ring Ken. We've got enough time if you want a shower before you put your dress back on. Then I'll drop you at yours so you can change into your gear and pick up Byron.' He smiled wryly. 'Those shoes you were wearing are pretty, but I don't think they're quite practical for a rescue search. And your dress might be a tad cold.'

'Mmm.'

'I'll give you space. Help yourself to whatever you need in the bathroom—which is next door, by the way, and the towels are fresh,' he said, and climbed out of the bed. 'I'll leave your dress outside the bathroom door.

Emma knew she shouldn't stare. She really knew she shouldn't. And yet she couldn't force herself to avert her gaze. Rob was just beautiful, naked. In perfect proportion.

But he wasn't hers.

Could be.

If she was brave enough.

But she wasn't. So she was just going to have to squash her libido.

When he'd grabbed some things from the wardrobe and the chest of drawers and closed the door behind him, she slid out of the bed and straightened the duvet. She would've collected her clothes, except most of them were in the living room. Along with her handbag.

Maybe Rob would leave it with her dress, outside the bathroom door.

When she opened the bedroom door, intending to head for the shower, her dress and bra were folded neatly outside, along with her handbag.

The man was a mind-reader.

Or maybe more thoughtful than the men in her life since her father's death.

For a moment she wavered. Maybe this could work out. Maybe she should be brave and try.

But she knew that the chances were she'd be setting herself up to repeat the same mistake she had with Damien. The same mistake her sister had made with Jonathan. Relying on someone who wanted very different things. And she wasn't that stupid.

She checked her voicemail, and returned Ken's call to say she was available and on her way; then had a very quick shower, and changed back into her clothes.

When she emerged from the bathroom, Rob was clearing things away in the kitchen.

'Um, do you want me to—?' she began.

'No. I was just doing this while you were changing.'

He was wearing jeans and a fleece. She knew he kept his walking boots in the car, and assumed his waterproof was there too.

'Ready?'

She nodded, and followed him out to the car. It had been drizzling on the way to Rob's flat, but the rain had become a fair bit heavier. So had the wind, gusting to drive sheets of rain into them. By the time she got to the car, she was already wet.

Finding someone in these conditions wasn't going to be fun. But it was even more imperative that they found the missing person quickly—the rain and the wind-chill factor made hypothermia even more likely.

'Thanks for the lift,' she said when he parked outside her house.

He shook his head. 'Look, we may as well go together. I'll say I picked you up to save me getting lost.'

'You've got satnav. And that's what you told Ken.'

'Beside the point.' He waved a dismissive hand. 'And your car's locked in the garage. Get changed, fetch your boots and your waterproof, and I'll open the back of the car for Byron.'

She couldn't yell at him for being bossy, because she knew that what he'd said made sense. So she just did as he'd suggested, changing in record speed into jeans, thick socks and a fleece. She pulled on her walking boots and grabbed her waterproof, then collected her dog, locked the door behind her and ran through the rain to Rob's car.

It didn't take long to get to the rendezvous point, a car park near a well-known climbing spot, though they were the last two to arrive.

'Emma's on my way so it makes sense for us to travel together,' Rob said.

He'd probably intended to forestall a comment by Ken, Emma thought, but all he'd really done was draw attention to the fact they'd arrived together—and it sounded like an excuse. As if they had something to hide.

'What do we know about the missing person?' she asked.

'Arthur Willis, aged seventy-three. Has mild dementia,' Ken said, looking grim. 'Apparently he used to be a fell-runner. And now he's gone missing, his daughter thinks maybe he's got confused. He remembers the distant past better than the recent past—and she thinks he's decided to go on one of the routes he ran when he was younger.'

'So he's local?' Rob asked.

Ken nodded. 'In the sheltered housing complex a mile or so down the road. The last positive sighting we had was at half past two, when the warden called in to see him. His daughter rang him at six—and when he didn't answer she called the warden, who found him gone. They've searched the complex thoroughly and he's not there. So they called the police. As he's vulnerable and at high risk, the police called us out to search. We think this is the most likely place because it's the nearest.'

'Do we have anything that Byron can use to get his scent?' Emma asked.

Ken handed her a shoe.

'Excellent.' She crouched down and let Byron sniff it thoroughly. 'OK, boy. We need to find him.'

'Are you and Rob happy to work together on this?' Ken asked.

'Sure,' Rob said.

Emma wasn't so sure, but this wasn't the time or the place to make a fuss.

Ken handed them a map. 'This is your area,' he said. 'Got your torch?'

'And back-up batteries,' Emma confirmed. She took the radio and spare batteries from him.

Rob took the lightweight bivouac tent and half of the portable stretcher; Emma took the other half of the stretcher. 'OK. We're all set.' She barely even glanced at Rob. 'Let's go.'

There was a definite barrier between them again, Rob thought ruefully. Despite making love, achieving the ultimate closeness, she'd shut him out.

Because she didn't trust men?

Or because she didn't trust him?

'Emma,' he said quietly as soon as they were out of earshot, 'we're on a rescue. I'm not going to push you to discuss things here. We're professionals. A team. And finding Arthur Willis is our top priority.'

In the darkness, he couldn't see her face—even in the torch-light—but he'd just bet her expression was one of relief.

She didn't want to talk about what had happened between them.

And he didn't want to push her until he could work out how to persuade her to give him a chance.

Every so often they stopped to flash their torches in the usual signal and to blow whistles and call. But nothing broke the ensuing silence.

'Dementia is rough,' Emma said suddenly. 'On both the patient and the carer. Imagine waking up every day and not really being sure where you are, who all these people are around you, what you're doing there. The anxiety must be horrible.'

'And then, as the carer, you want to greet your loved one with a hug and kiss but they treat you as a stranger—they're suspicious of you and can't remember any of the past. Years and years of memories just lost,' Rob agreed.

'And if the long-distant past is so much more real to you, how easy it would be to think the present day's a dream. To think that if you just go for a walk on one of the routes you know like the back of your hand, everything will be fine and all the anxiety will go.' She blew out a breath. 'Poor guy. I hope we find him fast. Being out overnight in this sort of weather, at this time of year, with no shelter would be tough on anyone, but more so on someone elderly.'

She cared. She really cared. So although she'd started the SARDA work because of her sister and she hated climbing, for some reason Emma did the rescue work because she wanted to. Because she wanted to make things better.

He wanted to make things better, too. For her.

But would she let him?

An hour of searching, and there was still no sign of Arthur Willis.

Rob could virtually feel the tension snapping in Emma. And he didn't think it was just his presence: she was clearly worried about their missing person.

'We don't know when he set off,' Rob said quietly. 'It could have been any time between half past two and six. Say he went out while it was still light—say three o'clock. The care home's a mile away. It might have taken him twenty minutes to get here. And even given his age, he'd still walk faster in the light than we can in the dark. If he walked for even an hour before stopping, he could still be some way away.'

'Would the confusion prompt him to walk in the dark? Or would he try to get some shelter?'

'I'd go for shelter,' Rob said. 'You know the area. Is there shelter near here?'

'Not much. Bushes, trees. It's deeper into the gorge where he might get some shelter, but the sides are pretty steep.' Emma sighed. 'We don't know what he has with him—whether he has food, water, a torch—or what he's wearing. Even if he was wearing a coat, if it wasn't waterproof or he went a different way and fell into the stream…'

'Hey. We've only been out an hour. We've got a long way until we give up,' Rob said. 'Plus we have Byron and his amazing nose.'

The dog was able to search large areas in short spaces of time because he could pick up the scent—that meant the rescue team could rule out areas quickly where the dog wasn't finding any scent.

'Emma? Rob?'

The radio crackled. Rob recognised Alison's voice, manning the communications centre back at the team's base. 'Anything yet? Over.'

'Not from us,' Emma said. 'And clearly you haven't heard from anyone else either or you wouldn't be asking us. Over.'

'Sorry, love. Nothing else to report. Over.'

'We'll keep going,' Rob said.

A second hour passed, in relentless rain and wind. He wished he'd thought to bring a Thermos. A hot cup of coffee right then was the most inviting idea on earth. Well, the second most inviting, he thought with a pang. The most inviting would be to be curled up under the duvet in Emma's arms, warm and drowsy and far from the freezing rain and the biting wind. But that wasn't going to happen, and neither was the coffee, so there was no point in letting himself get distracted.

And then finally they heard Byron bark.

Rescue dogs were taught to find the casualty, then stay with them and bark so the human element of the team could trace their way towards the sound.

'You beauty,' Emma said under her breath. She radioed through to Alison. 'It's Emma. Search dog Byron has located missing person, over.'

The response was a loud 'Whoo-hoo!' followed by a request for their position.

Emma gave approximate coordinates. 'We haven't made contact with Arthur Willis yet so we don't know if he's conscious or injured. But, given how long it's taken us to get here, there's no way he can make it back to the road with us by himself. Over.'

'Agreed. Over,' was Alison's response. 'I'll get the helicopter team on standby. Let's hope the wind drops a bit. Over.'

'Thanks. We'll give you more details as and when we can.'

Byron was still barking. Bark. Pause. Bark. Pause. As the sound grew louder, Rob called out, 'Hello? Mr Willis?'

To his relief, there was an answering cry. Faint, and he couldn't make out the words, but at least there was a sound. Which meant that Arthur Willis was at least conscious. Alive.

CHAPTER ELEVEN

FINALLY they reached Byron, who stopped barking and wagged his tail madly on seeing Emma again. She dropped to her haunches and made a fuss of him, then gave him one of the treats she kept in the pocket of her waterproof. 'Well done, boy,' she said, hugging him.

The elderly man beside him had clearly tried to get some sort of shelter. He was sitting with his back to the gorge wall in a shallow depression, though it hadn't done much to shield him from the wind or the rain.

'Mr Willis?' Emma asked.

He nodded, blinking in the torchlight.

'I'm Emma and this is Rob. We're from the Fellside Search and Rescue Team, and this is my dog Byron.'

'Lovely dog.'

He sounded a bit drowsy and his breathing was slow and shallow. She'd bet his pulse was weak and slow, too, if she checked it: definite signs of hypothermia. Though at least he was shivering hard, which was a good sign. If he stopped shivering suddenly, it would mean that that his hypothermia had become more severe. 'He certainly is,' she said lightly. 'Now, you must be freezing.'

'No, no, I'm all right.'

Was he trying to be brave? Or was he at the point where he didn't realise just how cold he really was?

'There's not much shelter here,' Rob said. 'I don't know about you, Mr Willis, but I could do with getting out of this rain for a bit. I've got a bivvy tent with me, so I'll put it up.'

'And I'm going to tell the team we've found you safe,' Emma said. She radioed through to Alison. 'Emma here, over.'

'Go ahead, Em. Over.'

'We're with Mr Willis now. He's fine. Moderate hypo.' She gave the co-ordinates. 'Rob's setting up the bivvy tent. We're going to shelter there and try and warm him a bit. Over.'

'I'll tell the boys. Be with you asap. Over and out.'

Between them, Rob and Emma shepherded Mr Willis into the tent. Although he was wearing a coat, it was soaked through, which meant, Emma thought, it had lost ninety per cent of its insulation value and the wetness was also contributing to the hypothermia. 'You need to take your coat off,' she said gently. 'And your sweater's wet, too.'

'No, no, no.' Mr Willis wrapped his arms round himself. 'I can't undress in front of a lady.'

'Emma will turn her back,' Rob said. 'And you can borrow my fleece.'

'Then *you'll* be cold,' Mr Willis protested.

'My jacket's waterproof,' Rob said gently, 'and I'm wearing a T-shirt under the fleece. I'll be fine.'

Emma turned her back. The rustling sounds were clearly Rob undressing. She shivered, remembering the way he'd raised his arms to let her pull his sweater over his head just a few short hours before. The way he'd removed her clothes. The way—

'Emma, you can turn round now,' Rob said, cutting in to her thoughts.

Mr Willis was huddled in Rob's fleece. 'It's a fair bit too big for me, lad,' he said.

'I know, but at least it's dry and it'll help to warm you up again,' Rob said with a smile. He looked at Emma, and mouthed, 'His skin's cold and pale.'

They needed to start warming him up. But they also needed to take it slowly—if they tried warming him up too fast, his blood would rush to the surface of his body, reducing the blood supply to his heart and brain and potentially risking a heart attack or stroke.

'I'm going to wrap a blanket around you, Mr Willis,' Rob said. 'It's heat-reflective material and it'll help to warm you up gradually.'

'A hat will help, too,' Emma said, rummaging in her rucksack. 'There's a spare one in my bag. You're a climber, aren't you?'

Mr Willis smiled at her. 'I most certainly am.'

'So I don't need to tell you that you lose most heat from your head. You already know that—and that we need to keep your head and tummy as warm as possible.'

He looked faintly confused. 'Why am I here?'

'Because you've been lost for a little while,' Rob said. He exchanged a glance with Emma. Was the confusion part of Mr Willis's dementia, or was it because of the hypothermia? She wasn't sure either.

'I can't think what happened. I've never got lost before,' Mr Willis said, looking anxious. 'I know I can't climb any more, I'm too old, but I just wanted to go out for a bit of a walk. Get some fresh air.'

'This sort of thing can happen to anyone,' Rob reassured him. 'The weather changes and catches you out, then it gets dark quicker than you expect and suddenly you're not where you thought you were.'

'That's right, lad. And people go out wearing unsuitable clothes.'

Just like Mr Willis had, Emma thought, in a coat that wasn't waterproof and everyday shoes rather than the sturdier type needed for a long walk. Though maybe he'd gone out thinking he was dressed the way he'd used to for walking in the Peaks. 'I've got some Kendal mint cake in my rucksack,' she said. 'Have a little bit. It'll make you feel better.' The carbohydrates would also help speed up the warming process.

He grimaced. 'Thank you, love, but I can't stand the stuff.'

'How about chocolate?' Rob suggested, digging into his rucksack. Byron woofed and Rob smiled. 'See, the dog knows it's good stuff.'

'Even though he's not supposed to have it,' Emma reminded him. 'And don't let him sucker you into it.'

'A husband-and-wife team—that's good,' Mr Willis said, smiling and accepting the chocolate. 'My wife never liked going out in the Peaks. She'd never go with me if I wanted to go walking or climbing.'

Emma was about to deny that they were husband and wife, but Rob put a hand on her arm and gave a tiny shake of his head, just out of Mr Willis's vision. Of course. He was keeping the old man chatting to help assess his condition, and if Emma tried explaining the situation, it'd just confuse things.

'When are we going home for a cup of tea?' Mr Willis asked suddenly.

'Soon,' Rob said. 'But first, because you've been out here a long time and you're cold, we need to get you checked over and warmed up in hospital.'

'I don't need hospital. I'll be all right at home,' Mr Willis said.

'I'd be happier if you had a doctor check you over,' Emma said. 'We're both doctors, but we don't have the equipment we need with us to check you over properly here.'

'Fellside General's a good place,' Rob said. 'We both work there. And you're OK with us, aren't you?'

'Ye-es.' Mr Willis frowned. 'You can't get an ambulance here.'

Even one of the Land Rovers would find it tough going,

Emma knew. Besides, given Mr Willis's age and the hypothermia issue, they wanted him to get to hospital as fast as possible. 'That's true,' she said. 'But the helicopter will be here soon. They'll take you to Fellside.'

As if on cue they heard the clack-clack-clack of the rotors.

The radio crackled. 'Base to Emma, come in.'

'Emma here. Over.'

'The helicopter team is going to send down a stretcher and winch the patient up. Andy's your winchman. Over.'

'Excellent. Thanks, Alison. Over and out.'

Emma smiled at Mr Willis. 'You've got the best winchman in the Peak District to look after you.'

'What they'll do is lower a stretcher down—we'll help you onto it and they'll lift you up,' Rob said. 'The winchman will be with you to make sure you're all right.'

'Andy's a nice guy. I've worked with him for years,' Emma said. 'And I've been up on a winch before now. There's nothing at all to worry about—it's as smooth as going up somewhere in a lift.'

'They'll probably take you to the emergency department where Emma and I work, first off,' Rob said. 'Tell them you know us and they'll make sure you get a decent cup of tea.'

Mr Willis smiled. 'Thanks, lad.'

Andy's head and shoulders appeared through the opening in the tent. 'Hi, guys. Mr Willis, would you like to come with me?'

Rob and Emma helped the elderly man out to the stretcher, and helped Andy secure him properly.

'What about your clothes?' Mr Willis asked, looking anxiously at Rob.

'Not a problem. You can leave them for me in the emergency department. And if you're still in hospital tomorrow, we'll pop in and see you,' Rob promised. 'We're both on duty.'

Andy strapped himself onto the winch line next to the stretcher, so he could keep it steady on the way up to the helicopter. He gave the signal to be winched up, and Rob and Emma waited until the stretcher had disappeared into the helicopter and the aircraft had started to move off before taking down the tent.

Once they'd repacked everything, they trudged back to Rob's car. Although they could move faster on the way back, because they weren't searching for a casualty, it still felt like ages until they reached the car park. And both of them were distinctly cold and wet.

Ken was still there, with a Thermos of coffee. 'There's only one cup,' he warned.

'I can live with that,' Rob said. 'I just want something hot. And if you weren't male and already married, I'd ask you to marry me for giving me coffee!' He laughed, and made a gesture towards Emma. 'You first, Em.'

'Thanks.' She took a couple of sips of hot coffee, feeling the warmth spread through her, and handed the cup to Rob.

He took a couple of sips, too—from exactly the same place that she'd drunk from, she noticed. Just as his mouth had touched hers only a few hours ago.

The idea made every nerve-end prickle. And when he handed the cup back to her, she turned it round to make sure she drank from a different place.

'Good result. Well done, you two,' Ken said.

'Byron's the real star,' Emma pointed out.

'He certainly is.' Ken crouched down to make a fuss of the dog. 'Right. I'd better go and pick my wife up.'

'And I'd better drive you back,' Rob said to Emma.

They drove back to her place in silence, both of them too tired to talk.

'You'd better go and change out of your wet clothes,' Rob said.

Emma wriggled on the seat. 'Um, I would invite you in to change into something dry, but I've got nothing that'd fit you.'

No, but you could dry my stuff over the radiator and curl up under the duvet with me. That'd work just fine, Rob thought.

He schooled his face into a smile. 'Not a problem,' he said.

'I'll, um, see you later,' she muttered.

And that was it? They weren't going to discuss this at all? 'Emma.'

She stopped with her hand on the doorhandle.

'Where do we go from here?' he asked.

She shook her head. 'I don't know—I think tonight counts as our second date so that's it on your usual terms, isn't it?'

'No.'

She sounded surprised. 'How do you work that out? You went for a walk with me, and tonight you asked me over for dinner.'

'That walk wasn't a date—I was just passing, dropped in to see you and invited myself along. And tonight wasn't a date either, because we arranged it as friends,' he added. 'Strictly speaking, we're still at zero dates.'

'But we…' Her voice faded.

He knew exactly what she was thinking. They'd made love.

'Yeah.' He took her hand and kissed each fingertip in turn. 'And it was everything I dreamed it would be. And, as I told you earlier, I don't want this to stop. I want to see you, Emma.'

'I don't think I can do this, Rob.'

Taking a deep breath, and hoping he'd guessed at the right reason for her reluctance, he said, 'I'm not Damien. I'm not going to let you down.'

'I know that.'

'Then why? What's the problem?'

'I…I can't explain it.'

'Em, for pity's sake, I'm not a mind-reader!'

She flinched, and he could have kicked at himself for snapping at her. He took a deep breath in an attempt to push back the irritation. 'Try,' he said, deliberately making his voice gentle. 'Tell me what's wrong.'

She shook her head. 'I can't.'

'I'm not going to let you down, Em. I'm really not.'

'Don't you have a reputation to uphold—two dates and it's over?'

'That's an excuse, not a reason—and it's not valid any more anyway.'

'I can't do this, Rob.'

He still didn't understand why. But right now they were going nowhere. Around in circles, Making each other miserable. 'I'm too cold and wet and tired to argue now. But we're going to talk. Tomorrow. At work,' he warned. 'And we're going to sort this out once and for all.'

'Mmm. Thanks for the lift.' She climbed out of the car and let Byron out of the back.

Rob waited until she'd opened the door and was safely inside, then drove off with a heavy heart.

He knew now that Emma was the woman he'd been waiting for all his life. But how was he going to make her see he was the right one for her, too?

Right at that moment it was beyond him. He couldn't think of anything more than a warm shower, a hot drink and curling up beneath his duvet. In a bed whose pillows would still bear Emma's scent.

Oh, hell.

He just hoped she'd talk to him tomorrow. Tell him what was in her head instead of backing away. Give them a chance.

CHAPTER TWELVE

AFTER she'd dried off the dog, showered and had a mug of hot milk, Emma expected to be so tired that she'd fall asleep as soon as she crawled into bed. But she was wide awake. Thinking about what Rob had said.

I don't want this to stop. I want to see you, Emma.

How easy it would be for her to let herself fall in love with him. With that teasing smile, the sense of humour mingled with dedication to his job and the rescue team. Those blue, blue eyes. A body that had sent her own into meltdown.

I'm not Damien. I'm not going to let you down.

But even if she risked trusting him, even if he didn't let her down, there was still a problem. A darned good reason why she shouldn't let him into her life.

She owed him an explanation. And as hard as it would be, she needed to tell him sooner rather than later. She had to make it clear that she couldn't have a relationship with him.

When the alarm woke her next morning, she had a thumping headache. She gulped down two paracetamol with her coffee, took Byron for a brief walk, then headed for work.

'Morning,' Rob said.

'Morning.' Here definitely wasn't the right place to tell him. But she couldn't let him keep thinking that they had a chance.

Not when they didn't. 'Um, I was wondering if we could have lunch together today.'

'I'd love to.'

She hated herself for the way his face lit up. The relief in his eyes. Oh, dear. She knew that what she had to say was going to hurt him. Badly. But what choice did she have? If she left it, it would get harder and harder, and the hurt would get worse and worse. 'Not in the hospital canteen.' She really didn't want their conversation overheard. 'There's a café just up the road from the hospital.'

'Sounds great.'

'Better see the patients before they're queuing from here to Sheffield,' she said, forcing a smile to her face. 'Catch you later.'

She had no idea how she got through the morning. A couple of bad cuts that needed stitching, a toddler with a rash, a severe asthma attack and, heading towards lunchtime, a football player who'd been on the wrong end of a bad tackle and had a dislocated patella.

Which meant she needed assistance to get the kneecap back in position—she needed someone to extend the knee gently while she levered the patella back into place.

As soon as she twitched the curtain aside, looking for Kirsty, Rob materialised. 'OK?'

'Yeah. Um, is it mega-busy out there?'

'Lull before the post-lunch rush,' he said.

'In that case, want to help me put a patella back?' she asked. 'I need someone to gently flex the knee for me.'

'Sure.'

She introduced Rob to her patient, then handed the footballer a mask. 'It's going to hurt a little bit, but the gas and air should take the edge off it,' she said. She showed him how to use the mask and breathe in the mixture of nitrous oxide and oxygen. 'OK. What I'm going to do is stand here.' She positioned herself so she was standing on the lateral side of his knee. 'Dr Howarth here is going to gently extend your knee, and I'm going to pop your kneecap back into place. As I said, it'll hurt a little bit when I do it.'

'It already hurts.'

'I know. But, trust me, once it's back in place it'll relieve nearly all the pain.'

'OK. I'll grit my teeth,' he promised.

'Ready, Rob?'

He nodded, and as he extended the patient's knee, she held the knee gently and used both thumbs to lever the patella back in one smooth movement.

'Bloody hell!' the patient yelled as she pushed on the patella.

'Take a deep breath of the gas and air,' she reminded him.

He did so, then blew out a breath and groaned. 'Sorry for swearing.'

She smiled at him. 'Don't worry. We hear a lot worse than that in here. Especially on a Saturday night after the pubs have chucked people out.'

'You weren't lying to me. It really doesn't hurt as much,' he said in wonder.

'Of course I wasn't lying. Haven't you ever heard the saying, "Trust me, I'm a doctor?"' she teased. 'Right—I'm going to send you for X-rays, to check there aren't any fractures or complications, and then I'll leave you in the capable hands of the plaster room. You'll need to see the orthopaedic team in a day or so for follow-up, so I'll organise an appointment for you.'

'Thanks. This is the first time I've ever put my kneecap out.' He grimaced.

'Probably won't be the last,' Rob said. 'Dislocations like this tend to recur.'

'Are you talking from experience?' the footballer asked.

'No.' Rob grinned. 'My speciality's fractures. Big ones.'

'Playing footy?'

'Climbing. Fell off a mountain.'

The footballer shook his head. 'Mad. Absolutely mad.'

'That's what she says.' He indicated Emma.

And Emma could almost see the lightbulb glowing in the man's head as he worked it out. She and Rob were an item.

Oh, no.

Lunch was going to be awful. Really, really awful.

But if she didn't do it now, she was storing up a heap of misery for both of them.

She reviewed the X-rays after she'd written up most of her notes. They didn't show any signs of a fracture, so she booked an appointment with the orthopaedic team and sent the patient off to get a cast.

And then it was lunchtime.

Time to talk to Rob. To explain.

The streets were already crowded with people doing their Christmas shopping, but because they'd opted for an early lunch they were able to get a table in the café. Better still, it was in a quiet corner. Rob was pleased, because he knew that Emma was a fairly private person.

The seriousness of her expression worried him. But whatever the problem was, surely they'd be able to work it through together?

'What would you like?' he asked.

'They do the most fabulous soup here,' she said. 'And these things called "melts"—it's a big hunk of granary bread with whatever you want on it, Brie melted over the top and mango chutney on the side.'

'Sounds good to me. I'll go and order them. What sort of "melt" would you like?'

'Bacon, please.' She glanced at the chalkboard by the bar. 'And the carrot and coriander soup.'

'Drink?'

'Mineral water, please.'

'Back in a tick,' he said, and went to order their meal.

Her back was to him as he returned to their table, but he didn't like the set of her shoulders. Tension was coming off her in waves. He had a pretty good idea what she was going to say, and his heart sank. Maybe if he spoke first, he might be able to reassure her that he was serious. That he wasn't going to mess her around.

'So,' he said, sliding back into his seat. 'I know it's usually ladies first, but I need to start. I like you, Emma. I like you a lot.' Although it was more than that, actually. He'd been thinking about it the previous night. How he felt about Emma was deeper than he'd ever felt about anyone in the past. Even his ex-fiancée. 'I know I have this stupid reputation of never dating anyone more than twice, but I don't want it to be like that with you. And I *know* it's not going to be like that with you. The more I get to know you, the more I like you.' The more he loved her. But he knew she wasn't ready to hear that yet. He was going to take this one step at a time.

She was silent. Looked close to tears. He wanted to pull her into his arms, hold her close, tell her everything was going to be all right because he was there for her and always would be. But in a public place like this she'd squirm with embarrassment. Emma wasn't one for big, demonstrative gestures.

'Em. What I'm trying to say is I'm serious about you. I want you in my life. Not a temporary relationship. A real one. Yeah, it's scary. I never thought I'd ever say this to anyone, not after Natasha. But I want to make a go of it with you.'

She swallowed hard. 'I can't do this, Rob. I can't offer you anything else but friendship.'

He reached across the table and took her hand. 'Why? I know you've been hurt—and hurt badly—but you're not the only one. If I can take the risk, why can't you?'

'It's not going to work.'

'Why not?' He could feel his voice sharpening and hated himself for it. Yelling at her wasn't going to make her listen—if anything, it'd push her even further away. But it frustrated the hell out of him that she wouldn't give him a chance. 'I'm not Damien. I'm not Jonathan. What do I have to do to prove it to you?'

'It's not that.'

Her voice was so quiet, he could barely hear her.

And whatever it was, it had to be bad. Really bad. 'Then tell me, Em. Explain. It can't be so bad that we can't work it out together.'

'I…' She dragged in a breath. 'My sister. Lucy. You know she had motor neurone disease.'

He nodded. 'I wish I'd had the chance to meet her. From what you've told me of her, she was an incredible woman.' And her love and care had shaped Emma into the woman she was today: one with a strong sense of responsibility and duty and love. Emma *cared* about what she did.

'She was.' There was a distinct wobble in Emma's voice, and he increased the pressure of his fingers slightly, trying to tell her that it was OK, he was there and everything was going to be all right.

And, just at the worst possible time, the waitress came over with their meal. Rob released Emma's hand and thanked the waitress. As soon as the waitress had gone again, Rob said quietly, 'What's wrong, Em?'

'Motor neurone disease is hereditary.'

She was telling him that *she* had MND? He stared at her, shocked. What did he say now? What would she expect him to say or do? If he wasn't careful—really careful—this was going to blow up in his face.

MND. He'd never seen any signs of it. Could her doctor have

made a mistake? 'You have the edge on me here—I've never done a rotation in neurology, and you don't tend to come across many cases in emergency medicine. I don't want you to think I don't trust your judgement,' he said carefully, 'but are you totally sure about that? I thought nobody knew what the cause of MND was.'

She took a deep breath. 'Lucy had ALS—amyotrophic lateral sclerosis, which is the most common form. And there's a chance it's hereditary.'

'So you haven't actually been diagnosed with it?'

She shook her head.

Thank goodness. Although he hated himself for pushing her, making her talk about something that clearly hurt, he needed to know. 'But you think there's a chance you might develop it.'

'Yes.'

'How much of a chance?'

'Five to ten per cent.'

As if the waitress had some kind of radar telling her when customers were at the most awkward point of a conversation, she appeared to collect their plates.

'Was the food all right?' she asked anxiously.

Considering neither of them had eaten much, the reason for her fear was obvious. 'Yes, it was lovely, thanks.' Rob forced himself to smile. 'We ordered more than we could eat, that was all.'

She didn't look convinced. Oh, no. He wasn't in the mood for discussing it. He needed to talk to Emma. 'But I'd love a coffee, please,' he said. 'Em?'

'Coffee would be lovely, thanks.' She, too, was good at polite smiles, he noticed. Covering things up.

He had a feeling that he was the first person she'd actually told about her fears of developing MND. The fact she'd trusted him that much had to be a good sign.

It had to be.

Please.

When the waitress had finished clearing their table and left, Rob reached across the table again and took her hand. 'So how can you tell if someone has a hereditary form of MND or not?'

'Genetic markers.'

'What sort of gene are we talking about?'

'Autosomal recessive.'

He let out a breath. 'This might not be as bad as you think,' he said.

She frowned. 'How do you mean?'

'I got quite interested in genetics when I was an undergraduate. There are different sorts of genetic conditions—autosomal dominant, which means the condition will always be inherited; X-linked recessive, where women are carriers and can pass the condition onto half their male children; and autosomal recessive. If Lucy had the autosomal recessive gene, it means both your parents had to be either affected or a carrier because she'd had that particular gene from each of them.'

She nodded. 'Which gives me a one in four chance of being affected, a one in four chance of being unaffected, and a two in four chance of being unaffected but a carrier of the defective gene.'

Well, he should've guessed that she'd know that already. Apart from being bright, she was also perfectly capable of researching all the issues. 'So you already know the chances are you're not going to develop it. The odds are stacked on your side.'

'Of not developing it myself, maybe. Maybe not.' She sucked in a breath. 'But backtrack a bit. If it's the genetic form, I've got a two in four chance of being a carrier. Of passing the defective gene to my children. That's fifty per cent.' She shook her head. 'It's too high a risk. Damien—' She stopped suddenly.

Rob felt his eyes narrow. 'What?'

'He wasn't prepared to take the risk.'

'That's why he wanted his ring back?'

'That was the clincher, yes. He could just about put up with me looking after Lucy, though I think he'd have nagged me to dump her in a nursing home as soon as she became really ill.' Her voice was shaking slightly. 'But he didn't want it passed on to our children.'

Rob's fingers tightened round Emma's. 'And that was it? No discussion of other options—like adoption?'

At her silence, he gritted his teeth. 'Words fail me when it comes to your ex. I could throttle him for the damage he's done to you, Em. Yes, there's a fifty-fifty chance of you being a carrier—but only if it's the genetic form. And if there's a genetic marker involved, that means there's a test for it. Have you had it done?'

She shook her head.

'It might give you peace of mind, Em. Stop you worrying about whether you're a carrier or whether you're going to develop it yourself.' He paused. 'If you want to do it, I'll support you through it.'

She dragged in a breath. 'I'm not sure if I can face taking the test.'

'Em, there's a tiny chance you've inherited a double dose of a defective gene. A larger one that you're a carrier, I admit—but in the scheme of things it's still not that huge.'

'And supposing it's confirmed? Then it's going to be like a sentence hanging over me. At least this way I don't have to worry that every time I drop something, it's the beginning of MND.'

'I take your point, but do you really want to spend the rest of your life worrying when you don't have to? Look, is there any history of it in your family, apart from Lucy?' he asked.

'Not that I know of. But my parents were in their fifties when they were killed. They just might not have developed it yet. Or they might both have been carriers.'

'Or maybe Lucy's one of the ninety-odd per cent of people who just developed it and we don't know why,' he pointed out.

'But supposing…?' Her voice tailed off as their coffee arrived.

Rob could have throttled the waitress. Why couldn't they have gone to a café where the service was lousy and they were left to wait for an hour between courses? Even though right now he wanted to yell with frustration, it wasn't going to solve anything—a display of temper would draw attention to them and embarrass Emma, not to mention making her think that he'd go off at the deep end instead of supporting her when things got tough. So again he forced himself to keep his frustration under wraps, smile politely and thank the waitress for the coffee. And then he turned back to Emma.

'Supposing you get it or you're a carrier? Then we'll be very unlucky, but we'll deal with it. Look, when Lucy developed MND, did you think of her as a burden?'

'Of course not. But Jonathan did.'

'From what you've told me about him, he sounds like a self-centred fool and your sister deserved a lot better. Even if she hadn't had MND, he probably would have found some other pathetic excuse to justify having an affair, in his eyes. But not every man is like him. Look at your parents—they loved each other, didn't they?'

'Yes,' she admitted. 'But maybe they were the exception that proved the rule. Lucy picked men who let her down when she needed them. So have I.'

'Emma, if Damien had loved you enough, he would've made it work out. He'd have considered other options—like adoption, or fostering, or maybe egg donation and IVF if you both wanted to have a child genetically related to him. There are all sorts of ways around this.' And it still irked him that she was judging him by the same standards as Damien, and finding him wanting. 'I've told you before, I'm not like my predecessor at work.'

'I know,' she admitted.

'Good. Now you need to get something else into your head: I'm also not Damien. I'm not going to walk out on you over something like this.'

'I…I can't take that risk.' She dragged in a breath. 'I can't offer you more than friendship, Rob. For both our sakes.'

'I want more than that. And I'm not happy that you're trying to make the decision for me.'

'It's the right decision,' she insisted.

'No, it's not. It's based on guesswork. Firstly, you're assuming that those odds aren't in your favour. And, secondly, you're assuming that I'm going to be like every other man in your life to date and walk out on you when I'm needed most.' He raked his free hand through his hair. 'It's not an informed decision. Supposing you had those tests and it proved you had the genetic marker and would be likely to develop MND—*then* I'd be able to make an informed decision, because I'd know the facts. And you know what, Em? It'd be exactly the same as if you didn't have the marker. I want you.' He tightened his hand on hers. 'If you're a carrier, then fine—if you want children, we'll find another way of having a family together. And if it turns out you got the double dose and the choice is between having a little time with you and having no time with you at all, it's a no-brainer. I want you. That's not going to change.'

'I…' She swallowed hard, as if unable to tell him the fears crowding into her head.

'I know you're scared, Em,' he said, trying to keep his voice gentle. 'But you've trusted me this far. All it takes is one more tiny step.'

She shook her head.

'Why?' Frustration simmered through him. This was just like Natasha all over again. Natasha hadn't been prepared to look at the possibilities for their future: she'd just seen him as a potential cripple who'd ruin her life. In this case, Emma was convinced *she* was the one who'd ruin their future, not him, but the end result was the same—she wouldn't give them a chance. 'So you're not even going to try?'

'Don't push me, Rob. *Please.*'

Well, he had his answer. And right at that moment he couldn't bear to face her. If he stayed with her much longer, he'd lose his temper completely. Say something unforgivable. He released her hand. 'I guess you're right. If you can't trust me, it's not going to work, is it?' He pushed his chair up. 'I'm going to pay the bill. Stay and finish your coffee. I'll see you later.'

Clearly she saw the 'don't argue' signals in his expression, because she closed her mouth again without insisting that they went halves on the bill.

He walked back to the hospital alone. The idea of going back to the department wasn't an inviting one. Officially, he was still on his break, so he avoided the issue by going to the geriatric ward.

'Hi. Do you have an Arthur Willis here?' he asked the first nurse he came to.

'Are you a relative?' she asked.

'No. I'm one of the search team who found him yesterday. I wondered how he was doing.'

'Comfortable.'

Pretty much what he'd expected to hear. Rob smiled at her and showed her his hospital ID badge. 'Can I pop in and say hello before I go back down to the emergency department? I promised him yesterday that I would, and I'd hate to break that promise.'

The nurse smiled back at him, clearly reassured by the fact he was staff. 'Don't tire him out.'

'I won't.'

She told him which bed Mr Willis was in and Rob wished he'd thought to bring something. Not flowers, but maybe some grapes or a magazine. Too late now. He walked over to the bed. 'Mr Willis?'

'Yes?' The old man looked much frailer, sitting in a hospital bed.

'Rob Howarth. We met in the rain last night?'

Mr Willis frowned. 'Did we? What rain?'

'I was with Emma and her dog.'

Suddenly, the confusion in the old man's face disappeared. 'Lovely dog. Pretty girl, too. Nice voice.'

'Yeah, that's Emma.' The one he wanted to spend his life with—but who didn't want him. Who'd rejected him as thoroughly as his ex had. Which just went to prove he'd been right to keep all his relationships short. Commitment—or even the offer of it—meant heartache. He'd been stupid to think it'd be otherwise. He summoned a smile he didn't feel. 'How are you feeling?'

'Fine, lad. I'm going home with my daughter soon.'

'Yes, Dad.' A woman joined them at the bedside and hugged him. 'You're looking a lot better than you did last night.'

'Lad here lent me his sweater,' Mr Willis said.

'You were one of the searchers?' She smiled at him. 'Thank you so much. I was worried sick about Dad. If it hadn't been for you, he might have…' Her voice trailed off.

'Not just me. The rest of the team, too,' Rob pointed out. 'And the helicopter team, and the team who looked after your dad here.'

'I don't know how to thank you all.'

'No worries. It's our job.'

'He had moderate hypothermia, but he's well enough to go home this afternoon. Though he's going to stay with me for a few days first,' the woman said. 'I wish I could do it full time, but I can't look after him properly and work at the same time.' She smiled wryly. 'It doesn't matter that he doesn't always know me—he's still my dad and I love him.'

'I know what you mean,' Rob said softly. 'I feel the same

way about my parents.' And about Emma. But she wasn't going to let him that close.

And where they went from here…

Well, he already knew the answer to that.

Nowhere.

'I'd better let you get on,' he said. 'And I'm due back in the emergency department. Nice to see you again, Mr Willis.'

'You take care, lad.'

He forced a smile on his face. At least there would be a happy ending here. As for him—all he could do was hope that Emma would think about what he'd said. Learn to take that one last step.

But it wasn't much of a hope.

And he'd better get used to the fact that things between them were over.

CHAPTER THIRTEEN

WORK, that week, was a real strain. Emma was perfectly polite to Rob, but he was very aware that she was avoiding him—both in the emergency department and at the rescue team training night. The panto rehearsal was even worse, because Emma was really stilted and forgot half her lines. And she refused to go for the usual post-rehearsal drink, claiming she was tired and needed an early night.

Ken tackled him as soon as they'd sat at their table in the Crown.

'What's wrong between you and Emma?'

'Nothing,' Rob fibbed.

Ken stared at him with a 'don't give me any of that flannel' expression on his face. 'She's a lovely girl. And she's had a rough time of it. If you hurt her—'

'I'm not going to hurt her,' Rob cut in softly. 'If I do, you have my full permission to break every single bone in my body.' He sighed. 'If you want the truth, I love her.' There. He'd said it out loud now. Though he'd really wanted to say it to Emma herself. 'But she's not going to let me close. Not going to give us a chance.'

Ken frowned. 'How do you know? Have you told her how you feel about her?'

'Not quite,' Rob admitted. 'If I do, I think she'll run at a hundred miles an hour in the opposite direction.' He folded his arms. 'It's not going to have an effect on the panto or the team, I promise you that. We can both be professional about it.'

Ken didn't look convinced.

'We have to work together every day,' Rob reminded him. 'And here's the same: it's about the team working together to save lives.'

'All right. But the slightest hint of problems—'

'And I'll back off,' Rob said. 'Emma was here first. She knows the area, she's a fully paid-up member of the team, she has Byron. Of course she'll take precedence over me, and that's how it should be. But I'd like to think that both Emma and I are sensible enough to put the team first.' He stared into his glass. He wasn't going to break her confidence about the MND, but he was pretty sure they'd all known her long enough to know about Damien. And Jonathan. 'And maybe one day she'll realise I'm not like the men who've let her down in the past.'

Alison put a sympathetic hand on his shoulder. 'Give her time, love,' she advised.

Rob smiled wryly. 'I'd be prepared to wait for her for the rest of my life. Except she thinks I date people twice and drop them.' He sighed. 'She trusts me on a professional level. I just need to make her realise she can trust me on a personal level, too. That I'll never let her down.'

'If it makes you feel any better,' Alison said, 'she's smiled more since you've been around.'

A tiny flicker of hope blossomed in his heart. 'Then maybe…' He lifted one shoulder. 'But in the meantime I promise you I'm not going to put any pressure on her and I'm not going to do anything to disrupt the team.'

'That's good enough for me,' Alison said. She nudged Ken sharply.

'Me, too,' he said.

The following afternoon, Rob and Emma were both on a late shift when the ambulance crew radioed through.

'Suspected meningitis,' Rob said when he put the phone down. 'Headache, photophobia and a stiff neck.'

'Better get ready for a lumbar puncture, then,' Emma said.

'And make sure everyone's gloved and masked properly,' he added. 'If it *is* meningitis, it might be bacterial or it might be viral. We'll err on the safe side.'

At the handover, Keith couldn't tell them much about the patient's history. 'His name's Billy,' Keith said. 'The guy who called the ambulance thought he was just another homeless drunk in the park—but when it was obvious he was in pain, he got on the blower to us.'

Billy smelt as if he hadn't washed for weeks, but there were no alcohol fumes discernible.

'I've put him on oxygen, but his breathing's a bit irregular,' Keith said. 'Pulse fifty, BP a hundred and fifty over ninety.'

Even given that the older you were, the higher your blood pressure was, it was too high. And with the low pulse as well, that wasn't a good sign.

'Billy, can you hear me, love?' Emma asked gently.

The elderly man moaned, screwing his eyes shut against the light.

'You're in Fellside General Hospital,' she said. 'I'm Emma and this is Rob. We're going to look after you and make you feel better.'

Rob noticed that although they'd transferred Billy so he was lying on his back, his knees were drawn up. 'Can you tell me where it hurts?' he asked.

'All over,' Billy said, his voice raspy.

'Can you put your legs down so we can move you onto your side?' he asked.

Billy tried to put his legs down but moaned in pain.

'Kernig's sign,' he said to Emma. 'This looks to me like meningitis, but we can't do a lumbar puncture.'

'Why not?'

'High blood pressure with a low pulse and irregular breathing is a pretty good indicator of increased intracranial pressure. I want a CT scan—if the CT's clear, then we'll do the lu—' He was cut off by Billy going into convulsions.

'I need diazepam,' Rob said. 'Now.'

As soon as they'd stabilised Billy, Rob sent him for an urgent CT scan. To his relief, the results came back negative.

'OK, we'll do the lumbar puncture now,' Rob said. 'We'll need three bottles of cerebrospinal fluid for the lab.' He turned to Billy. 'We think you've got meningitis, Billy—that means the membranes covering your brain and your spinal cord are swollen and that's why you ache all over. I'm going to need to take a little bit of the fluid from around your spine so we can see exactly which bacteria might be causing the meningitis and give you the right drugs to cure it,' he explained. 'I'll use a local anaesthetic so it won't hurt, though some people have a bit of a headache afterwards.'

'Got a headache now,' Billy croaked.

'How long have you been feeling this bad?' Emma asked.

'Few days, few weeks.'

So the meningitis might not necessarily be bacterial: if the onset had been over weeks rather than days, it could be viral. Just in case, he'd send Billy for a chest X-ray after he'd done the lumbar puncture.

Emma and Rob gently rolled Billy onto his side, then drew his knees up. Rob cleaned the area where he wanted to insert the needle, at the base of Billy's spine, put local anaesthetic into the skin, then inserted the needle into the spinal canal and withdrew the cerebrospinal fluid. When he'd filled three bottles, he gently removed the needle and covered the puncture site with sterile tape.

'We're going to start you on some antibiotics before the test results come back,' Rob said. Meningitis could kill: early treatment minimised the risk of brain damage or death. 'Em, I need your local knowledge here. Do you know if there's much TB around here?'

'Haven't heard of a problem,' she said. 'Could be, though my guess is that it's caused by pneumococcus.'

'Right. We'll give him cefotaxime to start with, and if the bloods or CSF comes back showing something else, we'll change the antibiotics then,' Rob decided.

The chest X-ray showed clear reticulonodular shadowing and the blood results confirmed that Billy had TB.

'It's post-primary,' Rob said to Emma, 'so clearly Billy had it as a child and now he's got a compromised immune system from living on the streets, so it's reactivated. We need to change him over to rifampicin to deal with the TB.' His mouth compressed. 'Better test him for HIV as well. And I need to talk to the consultant in communicable disease control to sort out screening and tracing.'

'If he's been living on the streets, it's going to be hard to trace who he's been in contact with,' Emma said.

Rob nodded. 'CDC will have protocols there. But in the meantime we need to put him in an isolation ward, and he's going to need a prolonged course of treatment. We need to get checked, too, as do the paramedics and anyone who's been picked up in that ambulance since.'

He noticed that Emma looked worried.

'The chances of you picking it up are minimal,' he reassured her gently. 'We used masks in case it was viral, so that's going to help. But I can give you prophylactic rifampicin if you're really worried.'

'No, it's OK.' She shrugged it off.

Rob explained the situation to Billy while Emma sorted out

a bed in the isolation ward. And then he had the task of telling the CDC that there was a potential outbreak of TB—right at the time of year when people were socialising more than usual, visiting family and friends and going out to parties—before organising tests for Emma and the resus team, and Keith and the paramedic team.

'I've not been in contact with a TB case before,' Emma said. 'What happens now?'

'We take the Mantoux test. It takes two or three days before we get a result,' Rob said. 'The chances of us contracting TB are very small—and even smaller of it being infectious rather than latent TB—so you don't have to stay off work. You just need to be careful with the test site in your forearm, so you don't knock it or anything.' He knew she wasn't going to like the next bit. 'Which means probably not going out to a shout until we've been checked. Not because we could pass it on, but because there's more of a chance of you accidentally knocking the site when you're out searching in the dark.'

'You're just as likely to knock your arm in Resus,' Emma pointed out.

He sighed. 'Right now I don't have the energy to argue with you. Let's just get the test done.'

Along with Keith and the rest of the resus team, they gathered in the department while one of the CDC team came down to give them the test.

'It's a skin test,' the nurse explained. 'This is a purified protein derivative solution—it contains the TB antigens but not the live bacteria. I'm going to inject it just under the first layer of your skin, where it'll form a small bubble of fluid looking like a blister. You need to leave it uncovered and undisturbed, and don't use perfumes or other cosmetics. I'll come back and check it in forty-eight hours or so—if there's a raised red bump, it's positive and I might need to do more tests. It normally takes up to six weeks for the infection to show up, so I'd recommend doing this again in six weeks' time.' She paused. 'Have any of you had a recent viral infection?'

'Nope. Escaped the winter bugs, just to get this,' Keith said wryly.

'You don't necessarily have TB,' the nurse said with a smile. 'And nine out of ten people who've been infected with TB control its growth so only a few cells grow in the body. They're not infectious and they don't have any TB symptoms, but they have latent TB. That means if their immune system is compromised at a later date, the bacteria may grow again and they'll develop TB.' She looked at them. 'Anyone taking corticosteroids?'

There was a general murmur of negatives.

'Excellent. Last question: anyone had a recent live vaccine for mumps, measles, rubella, flu or chickenpox?'

'I had my flu jab back in September,' Keith said.

'Goes for us, too,' Emma agreed. 'Rob? You weren't here when the rest of us had ours.'

'I had mine in September,' he confirmed. And there was a warm glow in his stomach that she'd thought of him. Been concerned. Maybe there was hope. Maybe all she needed was time.

Two days later, the CDC nurse came back to check their skin tests. 'All clear,' she pronounced with a smile. 'We'll do another one in six weeks' time, to be absolutely sure.'

'Well, at least we can all relax a bit over Christmas,' Rob said.

'What are you doing over the holidays?' Emma asked.

Did that mean she wanted to spend time with him? He damped down the flare of excitement. 'Working over Christmas, but I'm off to Yorkshire for New Year to see my family. What about you?'

Emma shrugged. 'I'm working, too. I'll probably call in

and see my neighbours for a mince pie or something. And the canteen here does an OK Christmas dinner.'

Rob was tempted—severely tempted—to ask her to spend Christmas with him. OK, it probably wouldn't involve a traditional Christmas dinner as he wouldn't have time to cook it, but he could do something non-traditional for the two of them.

But the expression in her eyes warned him not to push it.

And what was the point, anyway? She clearly wasn't going to change her mind. Wasn't going to give him a chance.

He coped with the remainder of the panto rehearsals—including the dress rehearsal, when he'd never seen anyone look more beautiful than Emma did. The first two performances were fine. But in the last one his self-control splintered and the kiss went on way too long, to the point where Emma actually forgot her lines. Ken, as Buttons, ad-libbed swiftly and rescued the situation. And Rob really wasn't looking forward to the post-performance party: he knew the teasing from the cast would drive Emma even further away from him.

But maybe Alison had had a quiet word with the others after Rob's admission that he loved Emma, because nobody said a word. Just celebrated with champagne that they'd raised enough through ticket sales and donations so they could buy the equipment they wanted for the team.

Emma, Rob noticed, stayed as far away from him as she could. Though at least Byron came and sat with him.

'Sometimes I wonder,' Rob said softly to the dog, 'if waiting is the right way to go. If I should just pick her up in a fireman's lift and carry her off and to hell with tomorrow. But I don't want her temporarily. I want her for good.'

The dog licked him.

'Put in a good word for me, boy, eh?' Rob ruffled the spaniel's ears.

If only dogs could talk.

Rob's patience grew thinner and thinner. And then, on Christmas Eve, his mobile phone shrilled.

'Got a shout for another missing person,' Ken said when Rob answered. 'A kid who's run away from home after a huge row with his grandparents. You available for the search?'

'Sure. Where's the RV?'

Ken gave him the co-ordinates, and Rob scribbled them down before hanging up. He was tempted to call Emma see if she wanted to travel with him, but she had been staying out of his way since the final performance of the panto.

Give her time, Alison had said.

But how much time was enough?

When he got to the rendezvous point, Emma was already there. Ken dished out the areas—and Rob was teamed with Emma. She didn't look thrilled about it, but maybe this was what they both needed. Being forced to spend time together instead of running away from what was happening between them.

'At least he chose a mild, dry night to run away,' Rob said. 'Better than having a low cloud base or the kind of drizzle that seeps into your bones.'

'Or sheet ice. But even so, he could've slipped and fallen and hurt himself badly.'

As usual, she let the dog roam free to pick up the scent—the boy's mother had given them an old trainer for Byron to sniff.

And, after an hour of searching, Byron barked.

'Attaboy,' she said under her breath, then spoke into the radio. 'Alison, it's Emma. Think we've located him, over.'

'Thank God. I'll tell his mum. Where are you? Over.'

Emma gave the approximate co-ordinates. 'I'll give you an update as soon as we reach him. Over.'

But when they reached Byron, Emma's gasp was audible.

He was right at the edge of a drop.

CHAPTER FOURTEEN

'WELL done, boy,' Emma said, making a fuss of Byron and giving him a treat from the pocket of her waterproof. 'Hello?' she called down into the gully. 'Anyone there?'

'Here.'

The voice was quavery, but she thought that sounded more like fear than pain.

'My name's Emma—and you know that dog you heard barking?'

'He's stopped now.'

'That's because he's my dog. His name's Byron. His job was to find you and keep barking until I got here. What's your name?'

'J-Joshua. Josh.'

'Hello, Josh. Are you hurt, honey?'

There was a pause.

Oh, no. Please, don't let him be injured. Or, if he was, not badly.

'My foot hurts a bit.'

'Whereabouts are you?'

'On a rock.' Josh's voice was very wobbly now. 'A little one.'

'Do you think you can climb back up?' Emma asked.

'No-o. It's too steep, and I can't see. And my foot hurts.' Clearly more than just his brave statement of 'a bit'. 'I'm stuck,' Josh added, just to hammer the point home.

She grimaced and looked at Rob. 'The gully's known for it. You wouldn't believe the amount of times we have to rescue teenagers who decide to abseil down here and get stuck,' she said, her voice low. 'It's OK. I'm here with another of the team, Rob. We'll come and get you,' she called down to Josh. 'How wide's your rock?'

'It's a bit like a shelf. It's a bit bigger than my foot. But things keep falling off and dropping down.'

So it was a crumbling ledge? Oh, great, that was all they needed.

'We need to get a rope down to him,' Rob said, 'but if he's scared and he's not used to climbing and he's damaged his foot, I think we'd be better off going down to him and assessing before we get him up again.' He put his rucksack down and rummaged in it. 'Right—I've got my climbing helmet in my rucksack, plus a rope and belaying gear. If I set it up, you'll be in charge up here while I go down.'

Emma eyed the gully. 'You'll never fit down there.'

'It'll be a bit tight,' Rob admitted, 'but we can't leave him there.'

'I'm smaller than you are. I'll fit easier. Besides, you're heavier than me. It'll be easier for you to lower me down than for me to lower you.'

He frowned. 'But you hate climbing.'

He remembered?

'Are you sure about this?' he asked.

No. Not at all. But she mumbled something she hoped sounded like assent.

'Have you actually got climbing equipment on you?'

'No,' she admitted.

'Then you'll wear this.' He handed her the climbing helmet. 'There's a radio in it.' He switched it on, and took the other half of the radio out of his rucksack. 'Can you hear me, Em? Over?'

'Loud and clear. Over.'

'Good. That's working. I'll set up the anchor.' He called down the gully. 'Hello, Josh? I'm Rob.'

'Hello.' The boy's voice sounded quieter and quieter.

'I'm going to lower a torch down to you on a rope. I'm going to turn it on now. When I lower it down, you tell me whether I need to bring it more to your right or your left so it's nearly above your head, OK?'

'OK,' Josh quavered.

'Good lad. Here we go.'

Emma radioed through to Alison. 'Emma here. Over.'

'What's the situation, Em? Over.'

'Josh has hurt his foot—I'm not sure how badly—and he's stuck on a ledge in the gully. Over.'

'Not *the* gully? Over.'

'Unfortunately, yes. I'm going down and Rob's anchoring me. He'll be your radio contact until I'm back up. Over and out.' She handed the radio to Rob.

'I've got the torch down to Josh,' he told her. 'So we can see where he is now—you won't end up abseiling down on the poor kid's head.'

Abseil. Oh, lord. She was going to have to walk backwards over the edge. In the dark. With just a rope stopping her from plunging straight down the gully.

Emma fought to control her breathing. She could do this. Would do this. Lucy had done it often enough—so could she.

Even though it terrified the life out of her.

Rob finished sorting out the anchor and handed her the harness in silence. Once Emma had put it on, he attached it to his rope. 'Clear about what you're doing? Abseil down to him, assess his ankle, tell me what the situation is, and then we'll decide the best way of getting him up.'

No excuses. She had to do this. There was a funny little

pain in the area of her sternum, which she guessed was because of adrenalin. Her palms were damp inside her gloves, and she felt sick.

No excuses. There wasn't time to wait for another slender climber to go down. The ledge was crumbling. They had to rescue the boy.

'Want to know why I hate climbing, Rob?' she asked as she positioned herself at the edge.

'Why?'

'Because…' She took that backwards step. Oh, hell.

'Because?'

'I'm. Terrified. Of. Heights.'

And she'd just literally put her life in his hands.

Which ought to make her feel braver.

But it terrified her even more.

'Deep breaths,' Rob's voice said in her earpiece. 'You can do this. Take it slowly. One step at a time. I've got you, remember. You're anchored. You're in a harness. I won't let you fall.'

Jonathan had let Lucy fall. Damien had let her fall. How could she be sure that Rob wouldn't do the same?

'Slowly, slowly. I know where Josh is, so you don't look down. Keep walking. One step. One more. Keep going. You're doing great.'

'Doing well.'

He laughed. 'Nitpicking my grammar?'

Yeah. Because if she didn't do something, she was scared she'd either cry or wet herself.

'OK, honey. You're doing well. Call down to Josh. Ask if he can see you.'

'Can you see me, Josh? Flash the torch if you can.'

There was a flash of light against the rock. Excellent.

'Ask him if your bum looks big in that.'

'It does *not.*'

'Isn't this area where there are meant to be hundreds of dinosaurs?'

'No, that's Dorset. Lyme Regis.'

'Might be a mammoth down there. Keep an eye out as you're going down.'

'Robert Howarth, you're completely mad.' And she really couldn't understand how he could get a buzz from abseiling and climbing. She'd just bet he loved bungee-jumping as well and he'd leap out of an aeroplane if he had the chance. Whereas the height here made her stomach churn and the back of her neck was hot with anxiety.

'Jewels, then,' Rob continued. 'We're in Blue John mine territory. Hey, you might even discover a diamond deposit.'

'What, *here*?'

'Yeah, sure. Or rubies. Pearls.'

'Pearls aren't gemstones. Everyone knows they grow in oysters.'

'Emeralds, then. Or sapphires. Or peridots, the same colour as your eyes.'

'You're being silly, Rob.'

And then her feet touched the ledge.

'Oh! I'm here.'

'Well done.'

She realised at that moment why he'd kept up that nonsensical conversation. He'd deliberately been talking rubbish to distract her and stop her panicking, so she'd keep taking those tiny steps down without focusing on the drop below her.

And she had to blink back tears.

'Hey, Josh. I'm here now.' She wrapped her arms around the small boy—and right then she needed the hug as much as he did.

'So let me look at your foot. Show me where it hurts?'

He did, and she gently probed the front of his ankle.

'Ow!'

'OK, honey. I'm not sure if it's a sprain, badly bruised or a fracture. But we're getting you out of here.' She spoke into the microphone again. 'Rob. It's his ankle. I need a harness.'

'Coming down. Flash your torch so I can start it in the right place.'

She did. There was a shower of little pebbles. 'Coming down. Can you see it?'

'No-o.'

'I'm trying not to throw it down too hard! I need to anchor it up here, too. When I'm ready, I'll tell you. See the harness yet?'

'No— Yes. Edge of. Go to your left a bit. Bit more. Yes. Got it.'

She managed to strap the harness onto Josh, giving him a re-assurance she really didn't feel. She trusted Rob to get this right, but she was all too aware of the fact that they were on a ledge less than half a metre wide. A space that might feel wide enough on the ground but that felt incredibly precarious when it was all that was between them and a sheer drop of a couple of hundred feet.

'OK. We're ready when you are,' she told Rob.

'Tell Josh to count to three and he'll start to move up. Tell him not to worry if he swings about a bit, though I'll try and keep it as smooth as I can. By the time he gets to the top, Dave and Geoff should be here to help him over the edge.' He paused. 'You going to be OK to wait down there until he's at the top?'

'Yes,' she lied, and relayed Rob's instructions to Josh.

'Keep looking up,' he reminded her. 'Look up at the stars. See how many constellations you can name.'

'About three. Orion, the Plough and the Pleiades.'

That rattling sound… Oh, please. Please, don't let it be the ledge falling away. A little crumbling at the far end she could cope with. But what if it fell away completely?

Some search and rescue team member she was, wussing out like this.

'Stop it. Just *stop* it,' she whispered to herself.

'Stop what?' Rob sounded puzzled.

'Nothing,' she said hastily.

'What about Cassiopeia? The W-shaped one.'

'Can't see that from here.'

He kept her talking until he, Dave and Geoff had lifted Josh over the edge.

'OK, Em. Josh is safe and your exit's clear. You can climb up now,' he said.

Climb.

It'd be a lot easier, she thought, if her arms hadn't just turned to cooked spaghetti. No way were they going to support her weight.

'Em? Look up. Look for a handhold.'

'Uh-huh.' She could see a tiny, precarious piece of rock that was only a fingertip wide. It made the narrow ledge she was standing on feel like a football pitch in comparison.

'Reach up, honey. I've got the rope. You're *not* going to fall.'

'Uh-huh.'

'Emma. Listen to me. I'm going to talk you through it.'

'How, when you've never been down here?'

'Because,' he told her patiently, 'I've climbed plenty of places like it. Listen to me. You're not going to fall. You're going to walk up that rock, just like you walked down it. Except, instead of paying out the rope, I'm going to be taking it in this time. And every step is going to bring you closer to the top. Closer to home.'

Her breath shuddered. 'You fell.'

'And smashed myself up, yes. Because I took stupid risks. I don't do that any more. And with you I'm safety-conscious. More than safety-conscious. This is going to be just like taking Byron for a run in broad daylight. One step. Up you come. Reach for the handhold. It's there, and it'll bear your weight. Tiny little thing like you. Mind you, you did say your bum was big.'

She knew he was trying to tease her into forgetting the situation. 'N-not working, Rob.'

'It worked on the way down.'

'Not on the way up.'

His voice softened. 'OK. I can't bully or tease you up, then. So I'll talk you up. Can you see a handhold, just above your right hand?'

'Yeah.'

'Reach for it, honey. You can make it.'

'What about my foot? Where do I put that?' Her brain had turned to porridge. She couldn't remember how this was done.

'I'll take your weight on the rope. Don't worry. Just rest the tip of your foot against the rock. Handholds are what you need. One at a time. Now your left hand. Look up. The torch is on your helmet and it's a new battery. You don't have to worry about losing the light. Look just a little way above your left hand.'

'I see it.'

'Reach up. Hold on. OK?'

'O…' her breath hitched '…K.'

'Attagirl. Now your right. Look up. Find a handhold. Test it.'

He talked her up, handhold by precarious handhold. And slowly she began to relax. Realised she could do this. That it was fine. She could do this, because Rob was there for her. Guiding her. Encouraging her. He'd never, never let her fall.

And finally he was there, helping her over the edge. Wrapping her in his arms, oh, so tightly. And she was holding him just as tightly, her whole body shuddering.

'You did it. You were fantastic,' he told her.

'J-Josh?'

'Is fine. It's a sprain. Ken's sorting out getting him back to his parents. They're going to have a really happy Christmas now.'

'Christmas.'

'Yeah. Happy Christmas, Em.' His mouth brushed against

hers, and then it was as if sparks took hold, and she was kissing him back. Matching his passion.

'I love you, Emma Russell,' Rob said when he broke the kiss. 'I would've told you when you were climbing up, but I thought you'd dismiss it as the danger talking.'

'Isn't it?' she asked.

'Nope.' He kissed her again. 'After my ex, I didn't think I'd ever want to commit to anyone again. But you're different. Have been different, ever since the first moment I saw you.'

She dragged in a breath. 'Damien walked out on me. And Lucy's husband left her.'

'I've got news for you. Well, it's not news. You know it already but you're too stubborn to admit it.' He gave her a wry smile. 'But if I repeat myself ad nauseam, you'll get the message in the end. My name's not Damien. Or Jonathan. It's Rob. And I'm trying to walk *into* your life, not out of it. I love you, and I want to marry you. And that's not going to change. Not in a lifetime. I don't give a damn about genetics and risks. I want you in my life. Permanently. And just in case you missed that, I want to marry you.'

And then it hit her.

Rob was proposing to her.

In front of half the Fellside search and rescue team.

'Rob, I—'

'Not a word,' he said, resting a forefinger against her lips. 'I don't want an answer tonight. I want you to sleep on it.' He smiled wryly. 'Actually, that's not what I want at all. But my landlord would have a fit if I took you and Byron back to my place, and I'm not going to muscle in on your space. So the second-best option is for you to go home tonight and sleep on it. And we'll talk tomorrow.' He handed her radio back to her. 'Now, tell Alison you're safe before she sends out a second search party. She's been a bit worried about you.'

'Alison? I'm back up, so you can stop worrying now. Over.'

The radio crackled. 'Good. And I heard everything Rob just said to you.'

Emma felt the colour shoot into her face. 'Everything?'

'Yes. I'm not going to interfere. But I will say this: he's a good man. And your dog likes him. Think about that. Over.'

They packed up their gear and headed back to where they'd parked. She let Byron into the back of her care. 'I'll, um, see you tomorrow, then,' she said to Rob.

'Yeah. Sweet dreams.'

She knew what he was really saying. *Dream of me. Trust me. Tell me tomorrow you'll marry me.*

Take that one last little step.

Reach out.

Just as he'd taught her to do up that cliff.

Despite it being Christmas Day, they were surprisingly busy in the emergency department. Although Emma and Rob managed to get a break in the morning, it was literally just long enough for them to make a coffee, add cold water to it and drink it straight down.

'Want to have lunch with me in the canteen today?' Emma asked on their way back to cubicles.

'That'd be nice,' Rob said.

He was clearly trying so hard not to put pressure on her. And she loved him for it.

Loved him, full stop.

And it was about time she told him.

Because it was Christmas, the canteen gave them a cracker with their Christmas dinner. And Emma somehow managed to find a quiet table near the Christmas tree in the corner—a tree sparkling with tinsel and baubles, with a huge gold star at the top.

Weren't you supposed to make a wish upon a star? And with Christmas being a time of miracles, maybe it would all come true.

'Did you sleep well last night?' Rob asked when they'd sat down.

'Eventually. After I'd been thinking for a while,' she said.

The canteen was playing carols, very softly. 'Silent Night', Lucy's favourite. *All is calm, all is bright.*

Rob looked at her. 'This holds memories for you, doesn't it?'

She nodded. 'Always brings a lump to my throat. Mind you, when I was doing a rotation in Paediatrics and the kids started singing "Away in a manger", I think the whole staff started bawling.'

'Christmas is a time for smiles,' he said softly. 'A time for making memories. A time for sharing.' He held his cracker out to her; she pulled the other end. It was more of a pop than a bang, but the cracker broke and spilled its contents between them.

A joke, a hat—and a plastic ring.

Rob's eyes glittered. 'Now, I would say that was fate, rather than coincidence.'

'Maybe.'

'Definitely,' he corrected. 'And I'm taking it as a sign to be brave. This is a Christmas gift, Em.' To her surprise, he dropped to one knee. 'Will you do me the honour of becoming my wife, Emma Russell? Though right now I admit I can't offer you anything better than a plastic ring from a cracker and a promise to love you for the rest of my life.'

Gently, she took his hand. 'And you're a man who keeps his promises.'

'Yes.'

'And I've already kept you waiting for an answer.'

He lifted a shoulder. 'You've already taught me to be patient. I can wait until the answer's yes.'

'So the party animal's gone?'

'No. The party animal and the climber are still there,' he corrected. 'But the only person they want to date is you. And your dog. And, if you want children—whether they're our own or adopted—them, too.'

She smiled. 'Something I ought to tell you, Robert Howarth. It's taken me a long while to let myself realise it, but I love you. And I'd be honoured to be your wife.'

He climbed to his feet and pulled her into his arms in the same movement. 'So is that a yes?'

She grinned. 'That's most definitely a yes.'

And maybe it was her imagination, but the carols in the background seemed just that little bit louder: the long-drawn-out 'Gloria' from 'Ding dong merrily on high'.

'Hold that thought,' Rob said.

And then he kissed her.

EPILOGUE

Three months later

ROB stood in the tiny country church, hardly able to breathe.

In a few minutes' time he and Emma would be married. In front of all their family and friends. He'd taken her to meet his family at New Year and they'd immediately taken her to their hearts. Nearly everyone from the emergency department—except for those who'd drawn the short straw of being on duty—were there, and the entire Fellside rescue team, as well as Emma's neighbours.

His neighbours, too, since he'd moved in with her.

Please, let nothing go wrong now.

Emma had taken the test to see if she had the genetic marker for MND. Hadn't told him about it until the day her results had come. And then she'd asked him to open them for her. Trusted him to tell her the truth—and to be there for her whatever the results said.

And they'd celebrated the answer together. Negative.

No more barriers to getting married, in her eyes. Nothing she could pass on to their children—and they'd both discovered, the previous month, that they were broody. Wanted children.

He glanced at his watch. She should've been here by now. There couldn't have been a callout. All the search and rescue team apart from Ken were sitting in the pews on Emma's side of the church.

'Stop fidgeting,' his brother told him softly. 'She'll be here. Brides are meant to be late on their wedding day.'

'Three minutes is more than enough to make the point,' Rob grumbled.

'Stop worrying. She'll be here. She loves you.'

A split second later he heard the first notes of music—and sucked in a breath as his bride appeared. Supported on Ken's arm, wearing a long ivory dress and a lacy veil, she walked slowly down the aisle. Followed by his sister, his sister-in-law and his two young nieces. And on Emma's right-hand side trotted Byron, sporting a deep burgundy bow on his collar to match the bridesmaids' dresses and carrying the handle of a tiny basket in his mouth.

An important basket: the one part of the best man's duties they'd agreed to be non-traditional about. After all, the dog had been the main male in Emma's life for the past four years, and neither of them wanted the dog left out of their special day. So Emma had persuaded the vicar to let Byron be one of the bridal attendants.

The bridesmaids filtered into their pew, and the spaniel sat at Rob's feet, with the tiniest bit of direction by Emma. Rob smiled and took the basket containing the wedding rings from the dog, and then Byron went to sit at Alison's feet in the left-hand front pew. Leaving Ken to give the bride away—and Rob and Emma to exchange their promises.

'Dearly beloved,' the vicar intoned, 'we are gathered here today…'

Emma lifted her veil back and took his hand. 'I love you,' she mouthed.

Rob smiled, knowing that everything was going to be just fine. 'I love you, too.'

arms reaching around her to gather her back against his bareness.

On the wide bed they made love, not desperately as if they were short of time, not furtively as if they wished to keep their passion for each other a secret, but openly and joyously, holding nothing back, exulting in each other's physical attractions and finding new ways to reach the fulfilment of desire.

'It's better this way,' Kit murmured later when they lay close in drowsy contentment.

'Much better,' she agreed.

All negative thoughts had gone. Feeling secure in his embrace she thought about the future, the days and nights she would be with him, living freely and openly with him, no longer having to steal time from her own ambition to be with him, no longer feeling guilty because she had let passion overrule reason. She had made a choice, a passionate choice. She had chosen to love and be loved in return. The future looked bright. As bright as the sun at noon. As bright as the dazzle on the sea.

MILLS & BOON®

MEDICAL™

Proudly presents

Brides of Penhally Bay

A pulse-raising collection of emotional, tempting romances and heart-warming stories by bestselling Mills & Boon Medical™ authors.

January 2008
The Italian's New-Year Marriage Wish
by Sarah Morgan

Enjoy some much-needed winter warmth with gorgeous Italian doctor Marcus Avanti.

February 2008
The Doctor's Bride By Sunrise
by Josie Metcalfe

Then join Adam and Maggie on a 24-hour rescue mission where romance begins to blossom as the sun starts to set.

March 2008
The Surgeon's Fatherhood Surprise
by Jennifer Taylor

Single dad Jack Tremayne finds a mother for his little boy – and a bride for himself.

Let us whisk you away to an idyllic Cornish town – a place where hearts are made whole

COLLECT ALL 12 BOOKS!

Available at WHSmith, Tesco, ASDA, and all good bookshops
www.millsandboon.co.uk

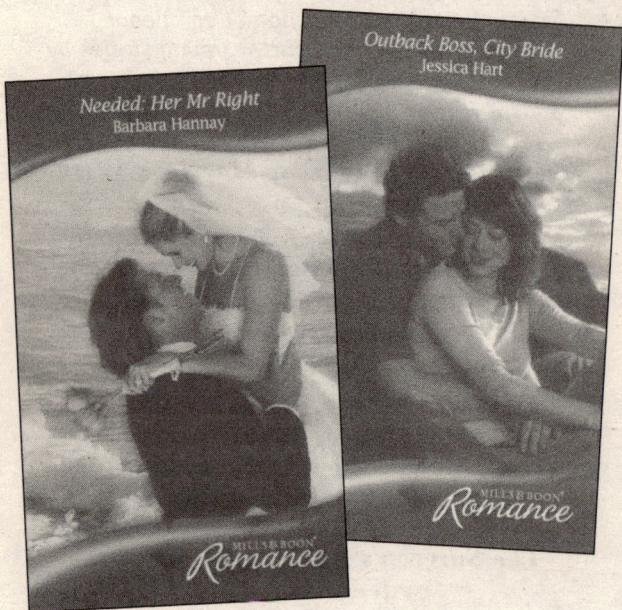

![MILLS & BOON 100 YEARS of pure reading pleasure]

100 Reasons to Celebrate

2008 is a very special year as we celebrate Mills and Boon's Centenary.

Each month throughout the year there will be something new and exciting to mark the centenary, so watch for your favourite authors, captivating new stories, special limited edition collections...and more!

FREE!

4 Books
and a surprise gift!

We would like to take this opportunity to thank you for reading this Mills & Boon® book by offering you the chance to take FOUR more specially selected titles from the Medical™ series absolutely FREE! We're also making this offer to introduce you to the benefits of the Mills & Boon® Reader Service™—

- ★ FREE home delivery
- ★ FREE gifts and competitions
- ★ FREE monthly Newsletter
- ★ Exclusive Reader Service offers
- ★ Books available before they're in the shops

Accepting these FREE books and gift places you under no obligation to buy, you may cancel at any time, even after receiving your free shipment. Simply complete your details below and return the entire page to the address below. You don't even need a stamp!

YES! Please send me 4 free Medical books and a surprise gift. I understand that unless you hear from me, I will receive 6 superb new titles every month for just £2.89 each, postage and packing free. I am under no obligation to purchase any books and may cancel my subscription at any time. The free books and gift will be mine to keep in any case.

M7ZEF

Ms/Mrs/Miss/Mr .... Initials ....
BLOCK CAPITALS PLEASE
Surname ....
Address ....
....
.... Postcode ....

Send this whole page to:
UK: FREEPOST CN81, Croydon, CR9 3WZ